**'Do you have an answer for me?' Rashad prompted, with an air of expectancy on his lean strong face.**

'Not yet,' Polly admitted, matching his honesty.

Polly's brain had flatly rejected marrying him at first. They barely knew each other, and it would be insane. *And yet*... She did want him—in fact she wanted him more than she had ever wanted any man—and she was not an impressionable teenager any longer. In fact, what if she *never* met another man who made her feel like that? That terrible feeling ... her hollow inside ... alive and wanted ... she had never felt before ... what was more, she was discovering that she *liked* the way he made her feel.

'Perhaps I can help you to make up your mind,' Rashad murmured with silken softness. 'You will see it as a form of blackmail, but in reality it is the only possible alternative if you do not wish to marry me.'

Polly's head reared up, blue eyes wide and bright. 'Blackmail?' she exclaimed in dismay. 'What are you talking about?'

# Brides for the Taking

*With this ring…*

At their mother's deathbed,
Polly and Ellie Dixon are given a name, a ring—
and news of a half-sister they've never met!

The search for their heritage leads these three sisters
into the paths of three incredible alpha males…and
it's not long before they're walking down the aisle!

Don't miss this fabulous trilogy, starting with…

*The Desert King's Blackmailed Bride*
February 2017

Continuing with Ellie's story…

*The Italian's One-Night Baby*
April 2017

And look out for Lucy's story, coming soon!

# THE DESERT KING'S BLACKMAILED BRIDE

BY
LYNNE GRAHAM

MILLS & BOON

First Published in Great Britain 2017
By Mills & Boon, an imprint of HarperCollins*Publishers*
1 London Bridge Street, London, SE1 9GF

© 2017 Lynne Graham

ISBN: 978-0-263-92395-7

Our policy is to use papers that are natural, renewable and recyclable
products and made from wood grown in sustainable forests. The logging
and manufacturing processes conform to the legal environmental
regulations of the country of origin.

Printed and bound in Spain
by CPI, Barcelona

**Lynne Graham** was born in Northern Ireland and has been a keen romance reader since her teens. She is very happily married to an understanding husband, who has learned to cook since she started to write! Her five children keep her on her toes. She has a very large dog who knocks everything over, a very small terrier who barks a lot, and two cats. When time allows, Lynne is a keen gardener.

### Books by Lynne Graham

### Mills & Boon Modern Romance

*Bought for the Greek's Revenge*
*The Sicilian's Stolen Son*
*Leonetti's Housekeeper Bride*
*The Secret His Mistress Carried*
*The Dimitrakos Proposition*
*A Ring to Secure His Heir*
*Unlocking Her Innocence*

### *Christmas with a Tycoon*

*The Greek's Christmas Bride*
*The Italian's Christmas Child*

### *The Notorious Greeks*

*The Greek Demands His Heir*
*The Greek Commands His Mistress*

### *Bound by Gold*

*The Billionaire's Bridal Bargain*
*The Sheikh's Secret Babies*

### *The Legacies of Powerful Men*

*Ravelli's Defiant Bride*
*Christakis's Rebellious Wife*
*Zarif's Convenient Queen*

Visit the Author Profile page at millsandboon.co.uk for more titles.

# CHAPTER ONE

KING RASHAD EL-AMIN QUARAISHI studied the photos
spread across his office desk. Six feet three inches tall,
he dominated most gatherings, having inherited his
grandfather's unusual height. Black-haired and possessed of long-lashed dark eyes, he had also inherited
the perfect bone structure that had made his mother
a renowned beauty in the Middle East. Indeed, his
smouldering dark good looks continually inspired admiring comments on social media and he was greatly
embarrassed by the fact.

'A cornucopia of feminine perfection,' his chief adviser, Hakim, remarked with fervour. 'A new reign, a
new queen and, we trust, a new *dynasty*! Truthfully,
fortune will smile now on the fortunes of Dharia.'

Although his royal employer appeared somewhat
less enthusiastic, he did not disagree. But then Rashad
had always known that it was his duty to marry and
father a child. Unfortunately it was not a project that
inspired him. After all, he had married before and at a
very young age and he knew the pitfalls. Living with
a woman with whom he might not have the smallest

thing in common would be stressful. Misunderstand-ings and personality clashes would abound in such a relationship and if the desired conception did not occur in record time the stress would multiply and the unhap-piness and dissatisfaction would settle in.

No, marriage held very little appeal for Rashad. The best he could hope for in a future bride was that she would have sufficient sense and practicality to enable them to live their separate lives in relative peace. He did not expect much in the way of support from a wife because his first wife had clung to him like super-glue. Nor was he likely to forget his parents' famously stormy marriage. Regardless, he also understood and accepted that the very stability of his country rested on his capacity to act as a respected role model for his people.

Over the past twenty-odd years the population of Dharia had suffered a great deal and change and in-novation were no longer welcome because in the de-sire for peace everybody had rushed to re-embrace the traditional relaxed Dharian outlook and customs. The heady years of his father's extravagance and his blind determination to force Western ways on an extremely traditional country had resulted in a government that became increasingly tyrannical and inevitably clashed with the army, who acted to defend the constitution with the support of the people. The history of that popular revolution was etched in the ruins of the for-mer dictator's palace in the city of Kashan and in the prompt restoration of the monarchy.

Tragically, a car bomb had killed off almost all of

Rashad's family. In the aftermath his uncle had hidden him in the desert to keep him safe. He had only been six years old, a frightened little boy more attached to his English nanny than to the distant parents he rarely saw and in the turmoil following the bomb and the instigation of martial law even his nanny had vanished. The palace had been looted, their loyal staff dispersed and life as Rashad had come to know it had changed out of all recognition.

'Your Majesty, may I make a suggestion?' Hakim asked.

Rashad thought for an instant that his adviser was going to suggest that he flung all the photos of potentially suitable brides into a lucky dip and chose blind. It would be a random form of selection and very disrespectful of the candidates, he acknowledged wryly, but he was cynically convinced that his chances of a happy union would be just as good with that method as with any other. Marriage, after all, was a very risky game of chance.

His wide sensual mouth compressed. 'Please...' he urged.

Hakim smiled and withdrew the file he carried below his arm to open it and extend it to show off a highly detailed picture of an item of jewellery. 'I have taken the liberty of asking the royal jeweller if he could reproduce the Hope of Dharia...'

Rashad stared at him in astonishment. 'But it is lost. How can it be reproduced?'

'What harm would there be in having a replacement ring created? It is a powerful symbol of the monarchy. It was the family's most important heirloom but after this long there is very little likelihood that the original ring will ever be found,' Hakim pointed out seriously. 'I feel that this is the optimum time to do this. Our people feel safer when old traditions are upheld—'

'Our people would prefer a fairy tale to the reality that my late father was a rotten ruler, who put together a corrupt and power-hungry government,' Rashad interposed with the bluntness that was his trademark and which never failed to horrify the more diplomatic Hakim.

While consternation at such frankness froze the older man's bearded face, Rashad walked over to the window, which overlooked the gardens being industriously watered by the palace's army of staff.

He was thinking about the ring superstitiously nicknamed the Hope of Dharia by the Dharian people. The ring had been a gorgeous fire opal of fiery hue, always worn by the King at ceremonial events. Set in gold and inscribed with holy words, the ring had acquired an almost mystical aura after being brought into the family by his saintly great-grandmother, whose devotion to charitable enterprises had ensured that she was adored throughout the kingdom. In other countries a king might wear a crown or wield a sceptre but in Dharia the monarchy's strength and authority had rested historically and emotionally in that ancient ring. It had vanished after the palace had been looted and, in spite of intensive searches, no indication of the opal's whereabouts had ever been established. No, the ring was gone for good and Rashad could see Hakim's point: a well-designed replacement would undeniably be better than nothing.

'Order the ring,' he instructed ruefully.

A fake ring for a fake king, he reflected with innate cynicism. He could never shake off the knowledge that he had not been born to sit on the throne of Dharia. The youngest of three sons, he had been an afterthought until his brothers died along with his parents. He had been left at home that day because he was an excessively energetic and noisy little boy and that reality had saved his life. Rashad's massive popularity with the public still shook him even while it persuaded him to bend his own ideals to become the man his country needed him to be.

Once he had wanted to fall in love and then he had got married. Love had been glorious for all of five minutes and then it had died slowly and painfully. No, he wasn't in the market for that experience again. Yet he had also once believed that lust was wrong until he fell in lust many times over while he was finishing his education at a British university. Whatever, he was still grateful to have enjoyed that fleeting period of sexual freedom before he had to return home to take up his duties. And unfortunately home signified the rigid court protocols that ensured that Rashad was forced to live in a little gilded soap bubble of perceived perfection as a figurehead that inspired the most ridiculous awe. Yes, his people would enjoy the restoration of the ring and all the hoopla of dreams and expectations that went with it...but he would not.

* * *

Polly glanced at her sister, Ellie, and managed a strained smile as a middle-aged blonde woman approached them after their mother's short funeral, which had taken place in an almost empty church.

Both young women had found the ritual a sad and frustrating event. Ellie, who was two years younger than Polly, had no memory of their mother while Polly had vague memories of an occasional perfumed smiling presence while she was still very young. Their grandmother had raised the two girls and the older woman had passed away only a few months earlier. For more than ten years the Dixon sisters had not even known if their mother was still alive. That was why it had been a considerable shock to be contacted out of the blue by a complete stranger to be told of Annabel Dixon's passing.

That stranger, a volunteer at the hospice where their mother had died, Vanessa James, was only marginally more comfortable with the situation than they were, having frankly admitted on the phone that she had tried hard to persuade their long-lost parent to contact her daughters and speak to them *before* her death. At the same time she acknowledged that Annabel had struggled to make herself understood in the later stages of her illness and such a meeting could have been frustrating and upsetting for all of them.

'I've booked us a table at the hotel for lunch,' Vanessa James announced with a determined smile as she shook hands firmly with both young women.

'I am so sorry that we are meeting in such unhappy circumstances.'

Polly had never felt less like eating and she made an awkward attempt to admit that.

'It was your mother's last wish and she set aside the money to cover the meal,' the older woman told her gently. 'It's her treat, not mine.'

Polly's pale skin flushed red with embarrassment, her white-blonde hair acting as a foil to accentuate her discomfiture. 'I didn't mean to be ungracious—'

'Well, even if you didn't you would have every excuse to feel uneasy about this situation,' Vanessa remarked wryly. 'Let me tell you a little about your mother's last years.'

And the sisters listened while the older woman told them about the terminal illness that had begun to deprive their mother of independent life and mobility while she was still only in her forties. She had lived in a nursing home and had died in the hospice where Vanessa had got to know her well.

'That's so very sad,' Ellie lamented, flicking her red hair back off her troubled brow, her green eyes full of compassion. 'We could have done so much to help her…if only we had known—'

'But Annabel didn't *want* you to know. She was aware that you had already spent years nursing your grandmother through her decline and she was determined not to come into your life and become another burden and responsibility. She was very independent.'

The three women sat down at the table in a quiet

corner of the restaurant and rather blankly studied the menus presented to them.

'I understand you're studying to be a doctor,' Vanessa said to Ellie. 'Annabel was so proud when she heard about that.'

'How did she find out?' Ellie pressed. 'It has been years since she last contacted our grandmother.'

'One of your mother's cousins was a nurse and recognised Annabel a couple of years ago when she was hospitalised. She brought her up to date with family developments. Annabel also made her promise not to approach you.'

'But why? We would have understood how she felt!' Ellie burst out in frustration.

'She didn't want you to see her like that or to remember her that way. Having always been a rather beautiful woman she was a little vain about her looks,' Vanessa explained gently.

Polly's mind was wandering. Thinking of her sibling's studies, she was very conscious that she had never achieved anything of note in the academic stakes and had done nothing to inspire a mother with pride. But then one way or another, life had always got in the way of her hopes and dreams. She had stayed home to take care of their ailing grandmother while Ellie had gone off to university to study medicine and she was proud that she had not been selfish. After all, her kid sister had always been very clever and she had a true vocation to help others. She knew just how guilty Ellie had felt about leaving her to cope alone with their grandmother but, really, what would have been the point of *both* of them losing out on their education? At school, Polly had been an average student, only plodding along while Ellie streaked ahead.

'I did so hope that you were in touch with your younger sister and that you would bring her with you today,' Vanessa James remarked, startling both women into looking across the table at her with wide eyes.

'What younger sister?' Polly exclaimed with wide blue eyes the colour of gentian violets.

Vanessa surveyed them in dismay before telling them about how their sibling had gone into foster care when Annabel could no longer look after her. She was four years younger than Polly and apparently their grandmother had refused to take her in.

'We had no idea we had another sister,' Ellie admitted heavily. 'We really know nothing about our mother's life…well, only what Gran told us and that wasn't much and none of it was flattering. She certainly never mentioned that there were *three* of us!'

'When Annabel was young she led quite an exciting life,' Vanessa volunteered ruefully. 'She was a highly qualified nanny and she travelled a great deal and lived abroad for long periods. She worked for some very wealthy families and earned an excellent salary, often with lots of perks thrown in. But obviously when she had children of her own she couldn't take them to work with her, which is why you ended up in your grandmother's care. But when you were both still quite young, Annabel *did* return to London, where she tried to set up a childcare facility. She poured all her savings into it. She was planning to bring the two of you home to live with her. But, sadly, it all went wrong. The business failed, the relationship she was in fell apart and she discovered that she was pregnant again.'

'And she gave birth to another girl? What's our sister called? Why are we only hearing about her now?' Polly gasped, only a little touched by the news that the mother she had never known had actually once planned to raise her own children. Indeed that struck her as a very remote possibility because it had seemed to her as a child that she had a mother who ran away from responsibility. Even worse, her outlook was coloured by the reality that she and Ellie had been brought up by a woman who bitterly resented the responsibility of having to raise her granddaughters at a time in her life when she had expected to take life at an easier pace.

Their sister's name was Penelope Dixon and Vanessa had no further information to offer. 'I did approach social services but as I'm not a blood relative I wasn't in a position to push. One of you would have to make enquiries. Penelope could have been adopted but I understand that if that proves to be the case you could leave a letter on file for her should she ever enquire about her birth family.'

Their meals were brought to the table. Vanessa withdrew three envelopes from her bag. 'Your mother has left each of you a ring and I must ask you to take charge of your youngest sister's ring for her—'

'A...*ring*?' Polly repeated in a renewed daze of astonishment.

'And with each a name. I assume, your fathers'

names…although Annabel was very evasive on that score,' the older woman revealed uncomfortably. 'I should warn you now that I'm not sure that Annabel actually *knew* who your fathers were beyond any shadow of doubt.'

Polly paled. 'Oh…' she said, in a voice that spoke volumes.

'She wasn't specific but I did receive the impression that when she was living the high life, looking after her rich employers' children, she may…er…possibly have been a little free with her favours,' the other woman advanced in a very quiet voice of apology.

'Sorry…? You mean…?' Polly began uncertainly.

'She slept around,' Ellie translated bluntly with a grimace. 'Well, thank you for being honest enough to tell us that before we get excited about those names. But with that particular disease, I know that Annabel may have had problems accessing her memories and she may have become confused when she tried to focus on the past.'

The instant Vanessa handed Polly her envelope, Polly ripped it open, patience never having been one of her virtues. A heavy and ornate gold ring with a large stone fell out and she threaded it on her finger but it was far too large. It was, she finally registered, a man's ring, not a woman's. She peered down at the stone, which flickered with changeable hues of red, orange and yellow.

'It's a fire opal, very unusual but not, I understand, particularly valuable,' Vanessa proffered. 'It's also an antique and foreign made.'

'Right...' Polly muttered blankly, returning to extract the small sheet of paper enclosed in the envelope and frown down at it.

*Zahir Basara... Dharia.*

'My...my father may be of Arabic descent?' Polly murmured in sheer wonderment, because, in the most obvious terms, she looked as though she had not a drop of more exotic climes in her veins and indeed had been asked several times if she was from Scandinavia. 'I have heard of Dharia—'

'Your mother was a nanny in the royal household there...right up until the royal family died,' Vanessa volunteered.

And Polly immediately wondered if there was a connection to her birth name, which had been Zariyah and which was on her passport. Her grandmother had always called her Polly, having disliked her foreign name.

'I've got an emerald!' Ellie announced as if she had just opened a Christmas cracker, her whole demeanour suggesting that she had no intention of taking either ring or name too seriously.

'And the name?' Polly pressed with rampant curiosity, hoping that it would be the same as her own putative father's because at least that would suggest that the relationship had been more than a passing fling.

'Possibly a name of Italian extraction. I'll keep it to myself for now though.' Ellie dug the envelope into her bag with an air of finality but she was unusually pale. At Vanessa's instigation she also took charge of the envelope intended for their sister, Penelope. 'Maybe our mother *collected* engagement rings—'

'My ring is a man's,' Polly argued.

'Yes, but there could have been an intention to make it smaller,' Ellie pointed out calmly. 'I wish she'd left us a letter telling us about herself. Would it be possible for us to visit the hospice, Vanessa? I'd very much like to see where Annabel spent her last days and speak to the staff.'

And while the two other women became involved in an intense discussion about the hospice, the disease that had taken Annabel's life and the research that Vanessa's charity raised funds to support, Polly drifted off inside her head, something that she did frequently when her imagination was caught.

Just then she was thinking about the fire opal and wondering if it had been a symbol of love. Ellie was of a more practical bent but Polly liked to think she had, at least, been born to parents who had been in love at the time of her conception. Love between two people of different cultures would have been testing, she reflected, and perhaps those differences had become too great to surmount. Even so, that name in the envelope had sparked a mad craving inside her for facts about the country of Dharia.

Did she have Dharian blood running in her veins? Was it even possible that her father could still be alive? And that he might want to get to know her?

Polly had a deep longing to have a real parent. Her mother had virtually abandoned them and while her grandmother had not mistreated Polly and Ellie she certainly hadn't loved them. Polly thought it would be absolutely wonderful to have a parent who actually cared for her as an individual, someone who would celebrate her strengths and overlook and forgive her weaknesses.

'You're not charging off to some foreign country to make enquiries,' Ellie said drily, having perused her sister's ring and the name on the piece of paper and surmised exactly where her sister's fertile imagination was taking her. 'It would be insane.'

And Polly had never ever done anything insane, *never ever...*

No, she had not defied her grandmother when she had won a place at art college and the older woman told her that she couldn't take it up because it was her duty to go out and get a paying job to help support the household. While suitably employed in a lowly but enjoyable position for a charitable enterprise, Polly had contented herself with the outlet of evening art classes shared with other enthusiastic amateurs.

Polly had never been particularly adventurous, so she knew then with a sinking heart that it was very unlikely that she would ever get to visit Dharia. She didn't have the money for air fares or holidays, she wouldn't have the cash to chase up some father armed only with what could well prove to be as common a name in Dharia as John Smith. No, it was a dream and Polly knew dreams didn't come true unless you were willing to take risks and seize the moment...

Polly was aware of being stared at in the passport queue at the airport outside Kashan. It was the blonde hair, she thought ruefully, aware as she looked around her with eager curiosity that her pale colouring seemed rare in Dharia.

She was here in her father's country, she was finally *here* and she still couldn't believe it! Ellie had made it possible, taking on part-time work in spite of her heavy study schedule and insisting that she could get by for one term at least without her sister's financial help. Even so, it had still taken Polly months of saving to acquire sufficient funds for such a trip. Her budget was tiny and she would be staying in a little bed-and-breakfast establishment near the bazaar in Kashan. As long as it was clean, she would be happy, and if it wasn't clean she would clean it for herself.

Encountering another prolonged stare from a dark-eyed male, Polly flushed and wished she had braided her hair. When she went out and about tomorrow, she promised herself, she would put on a sunhat to cover her head. After all, Dharia wasn't a tourist-orientated country and was kind of old-fashioned. She definitely wouldn't be wearing the shorts and vest top she had packed, for while there were no veiled women around those she had seen wore unrevealing clothes with longer hemlines than were fashionable.

Finally she reached the head of the queue and handed over her passport. That seemed to be the signal for another couple of men to approach the booth and a split second later one addressed her. 'Will you come this way, please?'

To her bewilderment she was accompanied to the baggage hall to reclaim her luggage and then her case and her bag were taken from her and she was shown into a bare little room containing several chairs and a table. Her case and bag were then searched in her presence while she wondered why her passport had not been returned. What were they looking for in her luggage? Drugs? A cold shiver of fear ran through Polly even though she had nothing stronger than headache tablets in her possession. She had heard horror stories about people being strip-searched and when a female airport security guard entered, her slight frame stiffened into defensive mode. There was an exclamation as one of the men removed the fire-opal ring from her handbag and held it high where it caught the bare light bulb above and sent a cascade of colour flickering across the drab grey walls. The trio burst out into excited speech in their own language and seconds later the two men slammed out, taking the ring with them. The female officer stared fixedly at her and Polly breathed in slow and deep in an effort to calm herself.

'You are very beautiful,' the woman said, startling her.

A sickly smile pulled at Polly's tense mouth because she didn't know how to respond to that remark in such trying circumstances. 'Thank you,' she said finally, reluctant to be rude.

The minutes ticked by like a hammer slowly beating down on her nerves. Her companion answered her phone. Polly linked her hands together on her lap and wondered why they had all seemed so excited about the ring. Was it a stolen ring? Was that possible? But what sort of ring could possibly attract such immediate recognition when according to Vanessa it was not worth much money?

Another woman entered with a tray of aromatic tea. Polly's companion stood up and offered her a cup. It smelled of mint and her hand shook as she lifted the glass up to her tense mouth to sip the fragrant brew.

'Why am I being kept here?' she dared to ask then.

'We are waiting for instructions,' she was told.

'And the ring?'

Both women exchanged looks and neither made an answer. Polly was angry that her ring had been taken from her because she treasured it as her sole remaining link with the mother she had never known. When would her ring be returned to her? At the same time she was trying to take encouragement from the fact that she had not been strip-searched and that tea had been brought. It was a misunderstanding. What else could it be? She had done nothing wrong. But had her mother done something wrong years back in the past?

How was she supposed to answer that question? In many ways, her mother remained a complete mystery to her eldest daughter. Annabel had travelled the world in luxury to look after other people's children while abandoning her own to the tender mercies of her own mother, who had been a most reluctant guardian. She had, however, dutifully provided financial support for Polly's grandmother and her daughters for many years. When that support came to a sudden unannounced halt, Polly had learned a lot about how to live on a very tight budget.

The sisters had inherited nothing from their grandmother. She had left the contents of her house, all that she possessed, to her son, Polly's uncle, complaining bitterly that her daughter had ruined her retirement by forcing her to raise her illegitimate children. It was a label Polly had always hated, a word the younger generation rarely used because it wasn't fair to tag a child with something that they had played no active part in creating. But it was a word that had meant a great deal to her staunchly conservative and judgemental grandmother, who had been ashamed that her only grandchildren had been born out of wedlock.

While Polly agonised on the other side of Kashan, Hakim, who rarely moved fast, was positively racing down the main corridor of the palace in his haste to reach his King. His rounded face was beaming and flushed, his little goatee beard quivering. Rashad was in his office, working diligently as usual.

'The ring!' Hakim carolled out of breath, holding it high in the air like a trophy before hurrying over to lay it down reverently on the top of the desk. 'It is found.'

Rashad frowned and sprang upright, carrying the ring in one lean brown hand to scrutinise it in the sunlight pouring through the window. 'How was it found? Where was it?'

Hakim explained about the British woman being held at the airport.

Rashad's dark as jet eyes hardened. 'Why is she not in prison?'

'This must be carefully handled,' Hakim urged. 'We would not want to cause a diplomatic incident—'

'A thief is a thief and must be held accountable,' his King assured him without hesitation.

'The woman is young. She could not have been the thief. She has not been questioned yet. The airport police wished to first ascertain with the palace that the ring was the genuine article. There is great excitement in Kashan. Crowds are already forming at the airport.'

Rashad frowned. 'Why? How could word of this discovery already have spread?'

'The airport grapevine was most thoroughly aired on social media,' his adviser told him wryly. 'There will be no keeping a lid on this story—'

'Crowds?' Rashad prompted in bewilderment.

'The woman concerned is not being viewed as a thief but as the woman who has brought the Hope of Dharia home to our King. When I add that she is young and apparently beautiful…well, if you think about how your great-grandmother came to your great-grandfather and brought the Hope with her, you can see why our people are thrilled.'

But Rashad was still frowning. A large gathering of thrilled people could translate all too easily into civil unrest. He could barely comprehend his aide's fervent attitude to what was, after all, only a legend, polished up by the next generation to enhance and romanticise the monarchy and their alliances. 'But that was a century ago in another age and it was a set-up to achieve exactly what it did achieve…a marriage that suited both countries at the time.'

'It is dangerous to have crowds congregating at the airport. I would humbly suggest that you have the woman brought here to be questioned. It will keep the whole matter under wraps without causing undue comment.'

Rashad was thinking with regret of the old dungeons in the palace basement. He didn't think Hakim wanted the British woman put in the basement. He reminded himself that the ring had come home and that the woman was apparently too young to have been responsible for its disappearance. 'Very well. I suppose it will be interesting to hear her story.'

'It is a complete miracle that the Hope of Dharia has been returned to us,' Hakim declared fervently. 'And a wonderful portent of good events yet to come.'

Sadly, there was nothing miraculous about Polly's feelings as she was herded out of the airport by what looked suspiciously like a rear entrance as they emerged into a loading bay surrounded by crates. She was clammy with fright in spite of the presence of the female security guard but her rarely roused temper was also beginning to rise. She was a law-abiding, well-behaved traveller. How dared they force her to endure such treatment?

'You are going to the palace!' the woman told her in a voice that suggested that she expected Polly to turn cartwheels of joy at the news. 'It is a great honour. They have even sent a car and a military escort for you.'

Polly climbed into the rear passenger seat of a shiny white four-wheel drive. She linked her hands tightly together on her lap. Over twenty years ago her mother had been employed at the palace and now she was receiving an unexpected opportunity to see the place, she told herself, striving to take a more positive view of her circumstances. If she got the chance to ask questions she might even meet someone who *remembered* her mother working at the palace. Of course, that could only lead to a very awkward exchange, she acknowledged reluctantly. Had her mother slept around? Had she been involved with more than one man? And how on earth was she supposed to find *that* out without seriously embarrassing herself and other people? For the first time, Ellie's forecast that seeking out her father would be like looking for a needle in a haystack returned to haunt Polly and she resolved to keep her personal business strictly private until she was confident of her reception.

A military truck crammed with armed soldiers led the way out of the airport and Polly's nervous tension increased as a big crowd of people surrounded the convoy when it slowed down to leave the complex. Faces pressed against the blacked-out windows, hands thumped noisily on the outside of the car and there was a great deal of shouting. Something akin to panic briefly gripped Polly's slender frame and perspiration beaded her brow. She shut her eyes tightly and prayed while the car pulled away slowly and then mercifully speeded up.

The car drove down a modern thoroughfare lined with tall buildings and lots of people standing around, apparently there to stare at the car she was travelling in. There were masses of people everywhere and a surprising suggestion of a general holiday mood, she thought in surprise as people waved in a seemingly friendly and enthusiastic fashion as the convoy passed by.

They left the city of Kashan and the crowds behind to travel into a desert landscape empty of human habitation. Flat plains of sand ornamented with rocky outcrops stretched in every direction and in the distance she could see giant dunes. There was something about that view stretched taut below a bright blue sky and the burning sun that made her want to paint in a medium different from her usual dreamy pastels. Distracted, Polly blinked as the car purred through giant gates into a startlingly green and lush spread of gardens dotted with trees and shrubs and colourful flowers.

Ahead loomed a very old building that was topped by a variety of large and small domes and which spread in all directions in a haphazard design.

The door beside her opened and Polly eased back out into the simmering heat, her lightweight trousers and tee shirt instantly sticking to her dampening skin. It was incredibly hot. A single female figure stood beneath the huge entrance portico and as Polly approached she bowed very low and motioned a hand in silent request that she follow her.

Clearly, she wasn't under arrest, Polly reflected with intense relief, her curiosity flying as high as her imagination as she entered the palace, but her anger at the fearful uncertainty she had endured remained. They padded down a very long and very broad hallway lined with ornately carved stone columns. Her sandals squeaked as she trekked after the woman into the depths of the great sprawling building. They traversed a shallow staircase and crossed a scantily furnished large room towards French windows that stood wide open.

Oh, dear, Polly thought in dismay, back to the horribly hot outdoors and the unforgiving burn of the midday sun.

She walked hesitantly out into a walled courtyard and her companion departed. Water gushed down into a fountain overhung by palm trees. The tiles on the ground formed an elaborate pattern faded by time. Polly moved straight into the shade by the fountain, desperate for the cooler air.

A young woman in a long fashionable dress appeared and dealt her a small tight smile, sweeping a hand helpfully at the table and two chairs sited in full sun. Suppressing a groan, Polly moved closer just as quick steps sounded from behind her. The young woman immediately dropped down onto her knees and bowed her head. Polly blinked in astonishment and slowly turned round.

A very tall man with blue-black hair and eyes as keen as a hawk's surveyed her. The hunting analogy was apt, she conceded, because she felt cornered and intimidated. He emanated authority and danger like a force field. He was also, very probably, the best-looking man she had ever seen outside a modelling advert and she knew who he was, thanks to her Internet research on the country of Dharia. He was the recently crowned ruler of Dharia, King Rashad. She swallowed hard, thoroughly disconcerted and shaken that she was being granted a personal meeting with such an important individual.

Her mouth had run dry and she parted her lips, struggling to think of something to say but he got there before her.

'I am Rashad, Miss Dixon. I would like to hear how the ring came into your possession.'

*I am Rashad,* she thought, as if there were only one Rashad in the whole world. And looking at him, she thought there might well only be one man quite like him in the Arab world, a remarkable man who had single-handedly united his country's different factions to bring about peace and who was universally and quite slavishly adored for that commendable achievement.

'The truth is…there's not much I *can* explain,' Polly admitted shakily, for the instant she connected with those striking dark brown eyes as luminescent as liquid gold in the sunlight she could barely breathe, never mind think and vocalise.

# CHAPTER TWO

'PLEASE SIT DOWN,' Rashad urged in a harshened undertone because he was finding it a challenge to maintain
his normal self-discipline.

An instantaneous lust to possess was flaming
through his lean, powerful frame and the uniqueness
of that experience in a woman's radius thoroughly unsettled him. But then the woman in front of him was,
admittedly, quite exceptional. Polly Dixon was blin-
dingly beautiful with hair of that silvery white-blonde
shade that so rarely survived childhood. Her wealth
of hair fell in a loose tangle of waves halfway to her
waist. Her skin was equally fair, moulded over a heart-
shaped face brought alive by delft blue eyes and a sul-
try full pink mouth. She wasn't very tall. In fact she
was rather tiny in stature, Rashad acknowledged abstractedly, doubting that she would reach any higher
than his chest, but the ripe curves of her figure at breast
and hip were defiantly female and mature.

Polly gazed back at him, dry-mouthed with nervous tension. He had amazing cheekbones, a perfect
narrow-bridged nose and a full wide sensual mouth en-

hanced by the dark shadow of stubble already visible on his bronzed skin. With difficulty she recollected her thoughts and spoke up. 'I gather all this fuss is about the ring that I had in my bag,' she assumed. 'I'm afraid I know very little about it. It only recently came into my possession after my mother died and I think that she had had it for a long time—'

Rashad's sister-in-law, Hayat, brought tea to the table, acting as a discreet chaperone and stepping back out of view.

'What was your mother's name?' Rashad enquired, watching Polly lick a drop of mint tea off her lower lip and imagining that tiny pink tongue flicking against his own flesh with such driving and colourful immediacy that he was glad of the table that concealed the all too masculine swelling at his groin.

Polly was starting to feel incredibly tired as well as desperately thirsty and she sipped constantly at the tea, wishing that it were cold enough to gulp down. 'Annabel Dixon,' she admitted heavily. 'But I don't see what that—'

Rashad had frozen into position. Lush black lashes swooped down to hide his eyes and then skimmed upward again to frame startled gold chips of enquiry, his surprise unconcealed. 'When I was a child I had a nanny called Annabel Dixon,' he revealed flatly. 'Are you saying that that woman was your mother?'

'Yes…but I know very little about her and nothing at all about her time here in Dharia because I was brought up by my grandmother, not by my mother,' Polly told him grudgingly while marvelling at the idea that her mother had looked after Rashad as a little boy. 'Why is the ring so important?'

'It is the ceremonial ring of the Kings of Dharia, a symbol of their right to rule,' Rashad explained. 'It has great emotional significance for my people. The ring went missing over twenty-five years ago when my family died and the dictator Arak staged a coup to take power here. Who is your father?'

Polly stiffened at his question. A headache was forming behind her brow and she was wishing she had access to the medication in her case while also dimly wondering when she could hope to be reunited with her luggage. 'I don't know but if all this happened twenty-five years ago it must've happened around the time I was conceived, so you see I have no further information to offer. I had no idea the ring was a lost treasure, nor do I know how my mother got hold of it or why she kept it. Surely she would've known how important it was?'

'I would've assumed so,' Rashad conceded. 'I was in her care with my brothers from birth to the age of six and during that period your mother must have learned a great deal about my family.'

'What was she like?' Polly was betrayed into asking.

He looked at her in surprise.

'I don't really remember her…at least I have only the vaguest of recollections. Perhaps you don't remember anything about her,' Polly added hastily, her very pale face flushing as she gave him that escape clause.

'She was always smiling, laughing,' Rashad recounted quietly. 'I was fond of her…as were my brothers. She was not blonde, like you…she had red hair—'

Polly nodded stiffly, thinking about her sister's red hair, which Ellie hated. 'Is there anyone else here who would still remember her?' she asked daringly. 'Naturally I'm very curious about her.'

'Few of the staff from that era remain in the household,' Rashad responded with regret, his lean dark face shadowing because so many of the palace staff had died in the coup.

'So what happens to the ring now?' Polly pressed tautly.

'It must remain here in Dharia,' Rashad pointed out in some surprise, as if she should have grasped that reality immediately. 'This is where it belongs.'

Polly lifted her chin, her blue eyes darkening with annoyance even as a mortifying trickle of sweat ran down between her breasts below her loose tee shirt. She might be feeling hot and bothered and impossibly tired but there was nothing wrong with her wits. 'But it is *my* ring and it's the only token I will ever have from my mother.'

Rashad was taken aback by her statement. 'That is most unfortunate but—'

'For me, *not* for you!' Polly interrupted fierily, her anger sparking at his immense assurance and his assumption that she would simply accept the situation.

Rashad was unaccustomed to being interrupted and even less familiar with the challenge of dealing with an angry woman. An ebony brow lifted at a derisive slant. 'You are more fortunate than you appreciate,' he told her levelly. 'You could have been accused of theft simply for having the ring in your possession—'

Polly rammed back her chair and stood up, bracing her hands down on the table to steady herself because that quick impulsive movement had left her a little dizzy. 'Well, go ahead and have me charged with theft!' she urged furiously. 'How *dare* you treat me like a criminal? My journey has been interrupted. I was marched off by security staff in front of an audience at the airport, held against my will in a nasty little room for hours and had the life threatened out of me when a crowd mobbed the car on the way here—'

'You were selected at random at the airport to be searched in a drug-screening scheme we have recently established,' Rashad interposed smooth as glass. 'I regret that you have been inconvenienced and embarrassed and will ensure that what remains of your holiday compensates you for the experience.'

Backing further away from the table and its support, Polly valiantly straightened her back and squared her shoulders to lift her head high. 'I want my mother's ring back!' she declared stridently.

Rashad rose fluidly upright, shamefully entertained by the sheer fury that had erupted in her face, flushing the skin to a delicious shade of pink, darkening her bright blue eyes to violet and compressing her lips into a surprisingly tough line. 'You must know that that is not true. The ring did not belong either to your mother or your family—'

'It was left to me. Therefore it belongs to me.'

Rashad raised a black brow as he strode towards

her and she warily backed away, her legs feeling oddly weak and unusually clumsy.

'The most basic law is that a stolen item may not be considered the legal possession of the person it is given or sold to because the individual who gave or sold it did not have the right of ownership to do so.'

Polly wasn't listening to him. After all, now he was talking like a lawyer and, even in his light grey designer suit, he looked like a fantasy against the colourful backdrop of the courtyard. He didn't look real, indeed none of what had happened to her since she first set foot on the soil of Dharia felt remotely real, so far did those events lie outside her experience. And all of it, *him*, her surroundings and the whole complex problem of the wretched ring, not to mention the heat, which she was finding unbearable, was becoming too much for her.

'I'm not going to discuss it with you because it's *my* ring, not yours!' Polly flung back at him dizzily while she wondered why her fantasy image of him was turning a little fuzzy round the edges and putting him into a soft focus that did very little to blur the hard cast of his lean, darkly handsome features.

'You are being most unreasonable,' Rashad told her without skipping a beat while he stared at her, fascinated by the firebrand personality hidden beneath that beautiful fragile outer shell. 'You are even being—forgive me for saying it—a little childish.'

Perspiration trickling down her forehead, Polly's small hands balled into fists. 'If you weren't who you are I'd thump you for saying that!'

A harried knock sounded on the French windows that led back into the palace and Hayat rose to answer it, bowing backwards out of his presence in the same way the staff had behaved over a century ago. The old ways were not always the *right* ways, Rashad reflected with a sigh. Polly shouting at him and threatening him with a ludicrous assault had had a wonderfully refreshing effect on his mood. Had she any idea how many Dharian laws she had just broken? No, nor would she care were she to be informed because she was angry with him and felt free to express her anger openly and honestly. Rashad had never enjoyed such freedom of expression or action. All he had learned about from the age of six was duty and the always dire consequences of *not* doing one's duty.

Hakim was framed breathless in the doorway, frantically indicating a need to speak to him.

Rashad suppressed his irritation at the interruption. After all, whatever good or bad thing had happened, it was his job to deal with it, regardless of mood and timing. For one final self-indulgent moment, he focused on Polly, marvelling at her pale perfection in the sunlight. 'I don't think you could hit me even if you tried to do so,' he responded silkily. 'I am highly skilled in almost every form of combat.'

'But you talk like a textbook,' Polly mumbled shakily, moving jerkily forward as if she was struggling to walk back to the table.

But she didn't make it. Her small frame crumpled down on the tiles in a heap. Hayat released a small startled scream but Rashad was a lot more practical.

He bent down and scooped Polly up off the ground, astonished by how little her slight body weighed. Hayat went from screaming to wailing an urgent cry for help indoors so that a squad of guards came running in an unnecessary panic that their King was in danger.

Rashad refused to put Polly down when others offered to release him from his burden. Hakim was already calling the palace doctor. 'I will speak to you when we are alone,' he murmured guardedly.

'What is the matter with her? Bad temper!' Hayat remarked to no one in particular in the lift, which was uncomfortably full of people. 'She shouted at the King. I could not believe my eyes or ears.'

Rashad wondered idly whether Hayat had been a playground sneak, who told tales on her peers. She was very snide about other women and always in his vicinity as if she feared he might not notice female flaws without her drawing them to his attention. He knew that as the sister of his late wife she regarded herself as a superior being. She belonged to a leading Dharian family. And every prominent Dharian family had put forward their daughters as potential brides for the King, a dangerous state of affairs that had convinced Rashad that he had to choose a bride from another country to maintain the peace between the various clans all jockeying for social position.

Rashad laid Polly down on a silk-clad bed. She was starting to recover consciousness, her eyelids flickering, little formless sounds emerging from her full pink lips. But even in that condition she contrived to look remarkably like an idealised image of an angel he had once seen in a book.

'Dr Wasem is here,' Hakim said at his elbow, and Rashad stepped back from the bed, suffering one of those weird 'moment out of time' sensations and momentarily spooked by it.

Being men, they retreated to the corridor while the female contingent of the household took charge.

'I wonder what is wrong with her,' Rashad said tautly.

'I wonder what our excitable crowds will make of this latest development. One of your guards used his phone in the lift. I frowned at him. He should have desisted immediately. What kind of discipline have we here when even the men dedicated to protecting you are taking a part in this media gossip nonsense?' Hakim was steadily working himself up into a rant.

'She was so pale. I should have realised it wasn't natural for her to be that pale,' Rashad breathed as if his adviser hadn't spoken.

Minutes later, Dr Wasem joined them. 'Heatstroke,' he pronounced with a hint of satisfaction at the speed of his diagnosis. 'Normally I would suggest our guest be taken to hospital but I am aware of the current mood in our city. The women will ensure that she is rapidly cooled down and rehydrated. I wonder whose idea it was to take a woman who had already endured a long flight outside during the hottest part of the day? Even our constitutions are taxed in such temperatures as we have in summer.'

A slight flare of colour outlined Rashad's stunning cheekbones. Sunstroke.

'That is serious—'

'Not as serious as what I have to tell you,' Hakim whispered once the doctor turned away to reel off further instructions to the cluster of women at the bedroom door.

With difficulty, Rashad rose above the guilt he was experiencing because sunstroke could be very serious and his guest could have had a fit, convulsions or even a heart attack if her temperature were not speedily reduced. He was appalled by his own thoughtlessness. 'And what is that?'

'Our guest may say she is called Polly but the name on her passport is Zariyah,' Hakim divulged in an even lower-pitched whisper.

'But that is…that is my great-grandmother's name. It is rarely used,' Rashad framed in shock, for the name was not used in Dharia out of respect for his ancestor's memory. 'How can her birth name be Zariyah?'

'My suspicions have taken me in a direction I really do not wish to go,' Hakim admitted heavily. 'But her mother's possession of that ring and her use of that name for her child, added to her unexplained disappearance all those years ago, deeply concerns me…'

'It is not possible that she could be a relative!' Rashad protested with rare vehemence.

'With the timing, added to your father's predilection for dallying with pretty women on the staff, it is sadly…possible,' Hakim spelt out grimly. 'A DNA test must be taken. Our guest could be your half-sister.'

'My...' Half-sister? Reeling with shock, Rashad had frozen into position by the wall as he struggled mightily to handle that shattering possibility while instinctively swallowing back any repetition of that familial designation.

That was not a result he wanted. No, he didn't want that, he definitely *didn't* want to discover that he had been sexually attracted to a long-lost family member. The very idea made him feel sick. But hadn't he once read somewhere about such unnatural attachments forming between adults who had not been raised together as children?

'It must be confirmed one way or another. We must know,' Hakim repeated doggedly. 'Annabel Dixon was a flirtatious woman and your father was—'

The strong bones of Rashad's bronzed face set hard as granite as he spoke. 'I *know* what he was.'

# CHAPTER THREE

POLLY SURGED BACK to recovery to find herself naked and being sponged down. In horror at her condition and the strange faces surrounding her she began to struggle to sit up and cover herself.

'I am sorry but this treatment is necessary to bring your temperature down quickly,' a pretty young brunette explained from the head of the bath in which she had been lain. 'I'm Azel and I'm a nurse. You are suffering from heatstroke and although this must be unpleasant for you, it is not as unpleasant as more serious complications would be.'

Heatstroke? Polly recalled the claustrophobic burning heat of that courtyard and suppressed a groan, knowing she should have admitted that she was far too hot out there. She was embarrassed by the fact that she had fainted and caused a whole fuss. Furthermore she had a vague memory of shouting at King Rashad and of threatening to thump him. Her cheeks prickled with mortification and she said nothing until the treatment was complete. The nurse took her temperature and blood pressure and pronounced both satisfactory before she was finally patted dry with a towel. She was then eased into some sort of silky garment and tucked into a very comfortable bed as if she were a young child.

An older man entered and introduced himself as Dr Wasem. He took a sample of her blood and a swab from her mouth before advising her to have a light meal and rest.

As if she were going to just lie there and sleep after all that had happened, Polly thought in disbelief. But once she had drunk as much water as she could manage her eyelids began to slide down as though weights were attached to them, her body sinking into the comfy mattress, and she was asleep before she knew it.

When she wakened, darkness had fallen and she focused in bemusement on the woman seated in a small pool of light near the door. It was Azel, the nurse who had addressed her earlier. Slowly she sat up and voiced her most pressing need. Urged to leave the bed with care in case she felt dizzy, she padded into the bathroom and freshened up with relief. It was after midnight and the silence within the palace walls was unfamiliar to a born and bred Londoner, accustomed to the sound of traffic and the outside glow of street lights.

A knock sounded on the door. 'Do you want anything out of your case?' Azel asked helpfully.

Grateful to finally be reunited with her luggage, Polly retrieved the necessities.

'I've ordered a light meal for you. You must be very hungry.'

'It's the early hours of the morning here,' Polly pointed out in surprise.

'The palace is staffed round the clock. It's a very convenient place to live,' Azel imparted with a smile.

A tray was brought and Polly tucked happily into a chicken salad. She wondered what time it was at home, not having yet got her head around the time difference. She would phone Ellie in the morning, she thought ruefully. In spite of her sleep, she still felt ridiculously tired and tomorrow when she got back to her inter-rupted holiday she would feel better able to explain how her unexpected inheritance from their late mother had brought her nothing but trouble. Her sister would be unsurprised, she thought fondly, for Ellie had a more cynical outlook on life than her older sister.

The next time she wakened, she could see the bright-ness of day lightening the wall above the curtains and she was alone. Rising, she dug clean clothes out of her case and she went for a shower. Well, this would be a tale to tell, she reflected with rueful amusement, flying out to Dharia in the hope of exploring her parentage only to end up spending the night in the royal palace.

A maid appeared with a trolley once she had re-turned to the bedroom and she chose a selection of foods from what was on offer and ate with appetite while she planned what she would say to her sister when she called her. She was reluctant to say any-thing that would wind up Ellie's fiery temper and more aggressive nature. Placed in the same position, Ellie would have been screaming for the assistance of the

British Embassy before they even got her out of the airport.

But when she dug into her handbag for her phone she couldn't find it even after emptying the bag contents out onto the bed. Her mobile had clearly been stolen. Her money was intact, as was her passport, but her phone was gone. She was furious. It was a cheap phone too, not one she would've believed anyone would think worth stealing. Well, she would take that up with King Rashad when she next saw him. In the meantime, she still needed to ring Ellie, who would be panicking because she hadn't got in touch when she had promised to do so. Honestly, even though Polly was older, Ellie treated her like such an innocent just because she had never been abroad before, Polly mused, shaking her head.

She opened the bedroom door and found a maid and an armed guard standing outside, which took her aback. She was even more disconcerted when the soldier wheeled round and dropped to his knees, bowing his head, muttering something in his own language. Well, good luck with that, whatever it was or meant, Polly decided, politely ignoring his display when it occurred to her that perhaps it was a prayer time of day and he was devout.

'I need a phone,' she told the maid. 'I have to phone my sister.'

The maid beamed and took her back into her bedroom to show her the landline by the bed. Polly suppressed a groan, not wishing to mention that she had wanted a mobile phone to make a free call on an app because she wasn't sure the young woman's English would be up to that explanation. With a sigh, reflecting that Dharia with its oil wealth could surely afford one phone call after the ordeal she had been put through, she lifted the handset.

Ellie answered her call at predictable speed. 'Where are you? Why has it taken you so long to phone me? I've been really worried about you!'

And Polly proceeded to give her sibling the watered-down version of the truth that she had already decided on but she did have to explain that their mother had apparently had no right to even have the fire-opal ring, never mind bequeath it to anyone.

'Well, I think a lawyer would need to decide that, not some jumped-up foreign ruler!' Ellie exclaimed, angrily unimpressed. 'You have to fight this, Polly. Are you sure you're free to leave the palace? Why have they a guard stationed outside your door? Try going for a walk and see what happens. I'm very suspicious about the set-up you've described and I think I may approach the Foreign Office to ascertain what your position is and ask for advice—'

'Do you really think that's necessary?' Polly prompted ruefully. 'Don't you think you're taking this all too seriously?'

'Polly…you don't pick up on warning signals!' Ellie condemned with heartfelt concern. 'You're always making excuses for the bad things people do…I'm not sure I could trust you as a judge of human character!'

Polly completed the call, her face flushed and sheep-ish. Now Ellie was up in arms and ready to do battle!

Although she believed her sister's concern was groundless she was willing to test Ellie's suggestion that she try going for a walk. She grabbed her sunhat and sunglasses and left the room, turning left at random and moving along a stone corridor, pausing to look down at an inner hall covered with the most eye-catching mosaic tiles she had ever seen.

She traversed a wide stone staircase and stilled again to admire a big wide corridor of elaborate arches that stretched away into the distance to frame the far vista of a lush garden at the end. As she set off to explore she noted that the guard was following her but not closely and he was so busy chattering to the maid that had accompanied him that Polly reckoned she could've turned cartwheels without him noticing. She wandered down the corridor and peered out into the gorgeous garden that shaded a pool in the shape of a star. The stone arches surrounding the courtyard were as exquisitely carved and detailed as handmade lace. It was truly beautiful and had she had her phone with its camera she would have loved to take photographs.

Her exploration ranged deeper into the building until she finally recognised the main hall where she had arrived the day before, and she was approaching the entrance when the woman who had served tea to her and the King appeared out of a doorway.

'Miss Dixon?' she called with a very artificial smile. 'The King asks that you join him for lunch.'

'How lovely,' Polly responded with a rather more natural smile, her face heating as she recalled her first meeting with Rashad, the gorgeous talker of textbook English.

Turning to follow the woman, she faltered only slightly when she finally registered that her guard of one had turned into a guard of six while she was wandering and all of them backed away in concert and flattened themselves back against the wall and averted their eyes as she passed by. Weird, *really* weird— maybe it was considered impolite to look too directly at a female, she pondered uncertainly. Certainly, her companion's jaw had tightened so much in response to that display that it might have been carved from stone.

Lunch was mercifully being served indoors, Polly appreciated as she entered a room with a polished marble floor and contemporary furnishings that fitted in surprisingly well with the ancient walls. Rashad appeared without warning, striding in through a connecting door to the left only to stop dead the instant he saw her. Her feet stopped too and without her meaning to still them where she stood. And there he was, she thought rather giddily, jaw-droppingly gorgeous and breathtakingly sexy. Sexy wasn't a word she normally applied to or indeed even *thought* of around men, but it rushed to her brain the minute she saw Rashad and it made her wonder if that was the main drawback of being a virgin and essentially inexperienced. Did sheer curiosity about sex give her a more impressionable response to men? But it had never happened to Polly around any other man, she reasoned, irritated by her wandering thoughts.

'Please sit here,' her companion interposed, tugging out a chair at the table Polly hadn't even noticed ahead of her.

'You look better today,' Rashad commented quietly as he settled down opposite her, his attention locked to the delicate colour in her cheeks and the sparkle in her blue eyes.

'Yes, feeling better too. Sorry about the fuss I caused,' Polly responded dismissively, trying not to look directly at him, utterly unnerved by the effect he had on her usual calm state of mind.

Rashad was disappointed that her hair was braided. He had never seen such beautiful hair before. Simply the novelty of different colouring in a country where most people had black hair, he told himself doggedly. She was wearing trousers again and a loose white top and he would not allow himself to wonder the things that his brain wanted to wonder. He angrily shut that side of himself down and began to make excruciatingly polite conversation of the sort he was accustomed to making at foreign dinner parties.

'My phone wasn't in my bag when it was returned to me,' Polly announced without warning, encountering eyes so dark they glittered like stars in the light filtering through the open doors behind him.

'Enquiries will be made on your behalf,' Rashad fielded smoothly, well aware that the phone had most probably been confiscated as a security precaution at Hakim's order. 'I am sure it will be found and returned to you.'

'Thank you,' Polly said equally politely, wondering why he seemed so different from the man he had seemed to be the day before.

He was more controlled, almost stiff and expression-less, the lean strong bones of his face cool and set, his jawline hard. Wary? Hostile? Offended? She marvelled at the extent of her own curiosity and scolded herself for it. Why should she care? She would soon be taking up residence in her little bed-and-breakfast place near the bazaar in Kashan and she could be fairly sure that she would never meet an actual reigning king again in her lifetime. He could only be lowering himself to shar-ing a meal with a foreign commoner to pursue the con-troversial topic of the fire-opal ring he wanted to retain.

'About the ring,' she began abruptly.

'We will not discuss that now,' Rashad decreed without hesitation. 'When you have fully recovered from your illness we will discuss it.'

Off-balance at the flat refusal, Polly studied him for several tense seconds. He was the most infuriat-ing man. She could see that he expected the subject to be dropped simply because he had issued an embargo and his sheer level of assurance hugely annoyed her. 'I *am* fully recovered,' she traded quietly. 'And grateful as I am for the care I received when I took ill and the hospitality which has been offered to me here, I would like to return to my holiday plans as soon as possible.'

'Perhaps we will discuss that tomorrow,' Rashad fielded without batting a single lush black eyelash.

'You do realise,' Polly whispered, because that hard-eyed brunette she couldn't quite warm to was seated only ten feet away, 'that you are making me want to thump you again? I thought it might be my high temperature that caused my loss of temper yesterday but I can now see that it was merely you being you—'

A brilliant smile unexpectedly stole the grim aspect from his lean, dark, brooding features. 'Me being me?' he queried with perceptible amusement in a clear encouragement for her to expand on her feelings.

'Horribly bossy. And I can see you're used to people doing exactly as you say—'

'Because I am the King,' Rashad filled in helpfully.

'But you're not *my* King.' Polly made that distinction with a slow sweet smile of mingled exasperation and reluctant amusement.

When he saw that smile, Rashad froze and leant back into his chair, squaring his shoulders while he wondered if she was flirting with him. Probably not, his brain told him. The British women he had been intimate with a few years earlier had used methods that were considerably more direct to attract and hold his attention.

'But you are still my guest,' Rashad retorted with lashings of cool. 'And the Dharian rules of hospitality are strict. One should never make a guest uncomfortable—'

'But you're doing exactly that right now!' Polly hissed at him in frustration.

His long brown fingers clenched taut round the cutlery. He tore his gaze from her lovely face, painfully aware that she made him very uncomfortable. With the discipline of years strengthening him, he studied his plate and he ate in complete silence.

'In fact, you're only making me want to stick a fork in you,' Polly whispered across the table.

And that was it—Rashad lost that minor battle. A wholly inappropriate laugh broke from his lips when he failed to stifle his enjoyment. Polly studied him in surprise and then encountered the brunette's chilling appraisal, which suggested that amusing the King could well be a capital offence.

'We will talk again tomorrow,' Rashad informed her quietly as they vacated the table they had shared.

Polly had to forcibly put a lid on her growing frustration with him. She was being too polite, she told herself. He had blocked her questions and refused to discuss the matter of the ring or tell her when she could leave. But did that really matter? After all, she was being treated like an honoured guest. Staying in the lap of luxury in a truly magical royal palace, another little inner voice chipped in gently, was scarcely a penance. It was a gift to be housed in such a gorgeous building, to be waited on hand and foot and to be wonderfully well fed. How could she possibly form a bad opinion of her host? It wasn't as though she had been stashed in some primitive prison cell. Moreover she was being granted an intriguing glimpse of a very different and far more colourful lifestyle.

Satisfied by that more positive take on her unexpected stopover in a royal dwelling, Polly wandered off to enjoy all that the exotic palace had to offer. She ignored the troop of men, armed to the teeth, and the maid following close behind her, and roamed from the magnificent desert views available from the recently built rooftop terrace down through the state rooms, with their superb intricate brass-covered arched doors and elaborate interiors, right down to the kitchen, with its army of busy staff, who fell silent and froze in shock when she first appeared.

With the maid acting as an interpreter, Polly ended up seated in yet another shaded courtyard, being plied with chilled strawberry and honey tea and an array of fantastic little pastries. Somewhere about then she decided that she was having a truly wonderful holiday even if it was not advancing her an inch in her unlikely search to find out more about her father.

Possibly that had always been an unrealistic goal, she thought in disappointment. Too much time had passed. How did she even risk voicing the name she had been given when the poor man might not be her father at all and was probably long since married? She didn't want to upset anyone and the mother she barely remembered had been sufficiently dysfunctional in her relationships even with her own family that she did not feel she could place much faith in Annabel Dixon's judgement.

Later that afternoon a dialogue that would have very much shocked Polly was about to take place. Hakim had collected the DNA results and had received such a shock that he had passed much of the afternoon at prayer, wrestling with his guilt and with sentiments it was too late to express. Having unburdened himself, he had then received a shock almost as great when events that had taken place a quarter of a century earlier were clarified for him by an unexpected source. Sharing that information with his King was almost more than Hakim could bear but he did not have a choice.

'Our guest is *your* granddaughter?' Rashad repeated with incredulity. 'How is that even possible, Hakim?'

The older man sighed heavily. 'At the time my son Zahir died we were estranged. That has been a lifelong source of regret to me. I was aware that he was involved with the nanny but I also suspected her of having other male interests on the staff at the time. I knew that my son wished to marry her and he refused to listen to my objections. I urged him not to marry her—citing the example of my own parents, who married across the cultural divide—and my son took offence.'

Rashad was silent while his trusted adviser unburdened his troubled conscience. Zahir had been Hakim's only child and that much more precious for that reason, and the day after the death of Rashad's family Zahir had died heroically trying to defend the palace and its inhabitants from Arak's squad of hired mercenaries.

'And now you see the consequences of my miscalculation. I spoke to my son from my head instead of from my heart. He loved this woman and she was already pregnant. He would not have told me *that*,' Hakim acknowledged hoarsely, his emotions roughening his usually steady voice. 'When the nanny vanished after his death I never thought about her again…why would I have? But I have only now learnt that Zahir married her privately and secretly only the day before he died. May I humbly request some time off to go home and discuss this astounding discovery with my wife—?'

'Of course,' Rashad breathed tautly, struggling to absorb the apparent truth that Polly, in spite of her misleading colouring, actually carried Dharian blood in her veins. 'But who does she resemble?'

'*My* mother,' Hakim confided tremulously. 'That hair. I should have suspected it the instant I laid eyes on her. I must also ask you to put all matters pertaining to my grandchild and the current unrest in the streets in the hands of my two deputies, because I am no longer a suitably independent and disinterested third party—'

'That I refuse to do,' Rashad responded instantaneously. 'I trust you as I trust no other man close to me.'

'You do me great honour in saying so but I—'

'Go home to your wife, Hakim,' Rashad urged gently. 'For today at least put family first and official duty second.'

Freed from the risk that Polly could be a half-sibling, Rashad smiled thoughtfully. Well, surprisingly, he was *her* King because although she did not know it her paternity granted her dual citizenship. He wished he could tell her that but it was her grandfather's right to break such news, not his.

The following morning other concerns swiftly consumed him when one of Hakim's aides brought the most popular newspaper in Dharia to him. The secret of Polly's true name on her passport was a secret no longer and it was just the kind of nonsense liable to inflame the superstitious with fanciful ideas. A single king, a single woman named Zariyah after his great-grandmother, the return of the Hope of Dharia… Such coincidences were being interpreted as supernatural signposts of heavenly endorsement in the home of his birth.

Rashad heaved a sigh. It was little wonder that Polly's birth name was now being chanted in the streets. He could not possibly let her leave the palace, for there was no chance of her enjoying an anonymous holiday after her passport photograph had been printed in the newspaper. Proving that the hysteria was generalised throughout every strata of Dharian society, the usually sensible editor had totally ignored all safety concerns when he put such information into the public domain.

And Rashad's day only darkened in tenor when he was informed that an official from the British Embassy was currently waiting to be seen. The diplomatic incident that Hakim had feared was beginning to happen…

Polly was watching the local television station as she ate her breakfast and wishing she could speak the language. She had tried and failed to access a European television channel. But she did not need Arabic to recognise that the massed crowds in the streets of the capital city were on the edge of overexcited. She wished she could read the placards some of them carried and waved along with the Dharian national flag.

Having promised to phone Ellie again, she did so. Her sibling startled her by admitting that she had spoken to a man from the Foreign Office and that official enquiries were being made about her so-called arrest and imprisonment at the royal palace.

'Oh, my goodness, Ellie!' Polly fielded in consternation. 'How could you *do* that? I'm having a really interesting time here—'

'This ring business you're involved in stinks to high heaven of some sort of a cover-up. I don't think you have a clue what's happening out there. As usual you're just sailing along and letting people push you around—'

Polly let her sister state her case and finally agreed that it was time she returned to the holiday she had booked and that she would *demand* the right to leave the palace and return to Kashan. Before she could lose her nerve she used the palace switchboard and asked to be put through to the King, wryly amused by her own daring.

'I have to speak to you,' Polly declared boldly as soon as she heard his dark deep drawl. 'And as I may shout, it would be better if we didn't have an audience.'

At his end of the phone, Rashad almost groaned out loud for palace protocol stated that he should never ever be left alone with a member of the female sex. He knew it was to protect him from the slurs and scandals caused by his father's debauchery but it was not easy to escape the tightly linked net of strict procedure.

'Meet me on the roof terrace,' he urged abruptly. 'I hear you were there yesterday and it is shaded. I'll join you as soon as I can.'

The strangest shred of compassion infiltrated Polly. It was clearly a no-no for him to meet up with her alone. When did the Dharian King ever get to be alone? She had seen the security team that followed him everywhere he went and she wondered what it was like to live in such a goldfish bowl where every word and every action was monitored.

Polly left her room and told the maid she wanted to walk alone. The three men guarding her room studied her in wonderment but when she moved off, she was not followed and relief spread through her because she felt really free for the first time within the royal walls with no one watching over her.

The shade on the roof terrace took what she believed to be a rather odd form. A giant tent had been set up at one corner. Within it opulent floor cushions surrounded a fire pit and there was an array of the implements she assumed were required to brew the traditional tea. Walking out of the bright sunshine, Polly sank down with relief on a cushion to enjoy the view. It was fifteen minutes before Rashad appeared through another entrance onto the terrace.

'We are breaking rules,' he told her with a sudden flashing smile of such charisma that her heart jumped inside her. 'This is not allowed.'

'Sometimes it's fun to break rules,' sensible Polly heard herself say dry-mouthed because for the first time Rashad was wearing traditional clothing, a muslin cloth bound by a gold rope hiding his black hair, a pristine white long buttoned robe replacing Western clothing. And that cloth merely accentuated his stunning dark eyes and arresting bone structure, so that breathing was barely an option for her as he sank with fluid animal grace down opposite her.

'And sometimes there is a price to pay for breaking

those rules,' Rashad murmured with wry amusement. 'Why did you want to speak to me?'

'I want to leave the palace and start my holiday,' Polly told him simply, even though she knew that somewhere down deep inside her she really didn't want that at all. It was the rational thing to do, she reminded herself doggedly. She did not belong in a royal palace.

Rashad linked long brown fingers and flexed them. 'I'm afraid I can't agree to that.'

He even had beautiful hands, Polly was thinking abstractedly before she engaged with what he had actually said and it galvanised her into leaping upright in disbelief. 'So, I *am* a prisoner here?' She gasped in horror that her sister could have been correct in her far-fetched suspicions.

'Do not lose your temper,' Rashad urged levelly. 'Allow me first to explain the situation we are all in—'

'The only person in a situation here is *me*!' Polly exclaimed angrily.

'There is great unrest in Kashan. You would not be safe…you would be mobbed. While no one would wish to harm you in any way, excited crowds are very hard to control.'

'I don't know what you are talking about.'

'Sit down, listen and I will explain,' Rashad instructed with quiet strength.

'No, you can explain while I stay standing,' Polly responded, determined not to give way on every point.

'Very well.' Rising as gracefully as he had sat down, Rashad stepped back out of the tent and strode over to the rail bounding the terrace. 'A century ago—'

*'A century ago?'* Polly practically screeched at him, gripped by incredulity that that could possibly be the starting point of any acceptable explanation for her apparent loss of all freedom.

'Close your mouth and sit down!' Rashad raked back at her in sudden frustration, his dark deep voice startlingly like a whiplash in the silence. 'If you refuse to listen, how can I speak and explain?'

Polly compressed her lips and sat down with a look of scornful reluctance on her heart-shaped face. 'Well, if you're going to shout about it—'

'I must make you aware of the most powerful legend in Dharian history. A hundred years ago, my great-grandmother, Zariyah, came to Dharia with the fire-opal ring and gave it to my great-grandfather, who then married her. My people think it was love at first sight,' Rashad advanced. 'But in actuality it was an arranged marriage, which was very popular and which ushered in a long period of peace and prosperity for Dharia—'

'That name,' Polly whispered with an indeterminate frown. 'Zariyah. That's the name I was given at birth.'

'The ring is also invested with enormous significance in the eyes of my people. The name on your passport was *noticed*. It may even be the reason why you were singled out for the drug screening process we have begun. You also brought the ring back to Dharia—'

'Not to give to you!' Polly objected vehemently.

'You are much given to interruption,' Rashad fired back at her rawly.

'And you are much given to being quietly listened to.'

'My country endured dark times for over twenty years. My people suffered greatly under the dictator, Arak,' Rashad told her in a curt undertone. 'They are very superstitious. Your appearance, your name and your possession of the ring has led to a hysterical outpouring of sentiment in the streets. At this moment in Kashan, people are waving signs bearing the name Zariyah because my great-grandmother was very much loved. If you left the palace, you would be mobbed and it would be extremely dangerous.'

Polly stared back at him with a dropped jaw. She could barely get her head around what he was trying to tell her. 'You mean, the coincidence of me having that name and the ring is sufficient—?'

'To cause all that excitement? Yes,' Rashad confirmed heavily.

Polly stared numbly into the fire pit, genuinely bemused by what he had explained. People were demonstrating in the city and waving those placards on her behalf? It was beyond her comprehension and her lashes flickered over blue eyes widening in growing amazement.

'But I don't understand. What do they want from me?' she queried numbly.

'In a nutshell, they want you to marry their King,' Rashad replied very drily. 'A single monarch, a single woman with the name of a famous queen…in their eyes it's a simple equation.'

'They want me to *marry* you?' Polly cried incredulously.

'And everything about you plays into their fantasy conclusion,' Rashad imparted with an edge of bitterness because the more he watched those crowds waving flags in the streets, the more his sense of duty warred with his brain. 'You are very beautiful. What man would not wish to marry such a beauty? And while you could have followed some inappropriate career as a stripper or a lap dancer, which would admittedly have doused their enthusiasm somewhat—'

'I beg your pardon?' Polly exclaimed furiously, jumping upright again.

'Instead you work in a homeless shelter helping the underprivileged,' Rashad completed. 'Yes, our media are every bit as given to spying as your own. You have been framed even in the newspapers as the perfect wife in the eyes of my people.'

Polly bolted out of the shade of the tent to stand by the rail in the golden sunshine, staring out at the lines of the shallow sand dunes gradually shifting into larger ones in the distance. 'I'm mortified—'

'I am trapped,' Rashad traded without sympathy, raging at the fates that had created such a disturbing and difficult situation. When he was crowned he had sworn to do whatever it took to make the people of Dharia secure and happy and he had never once considered that sacrifice of freedom as a personal constraint. Only now when it came to the question of his marriage was he finally appreciating the true cost of that pledge. But it also gave him a great deal to think over, he acknowledged, studying Polly and wondering what it would be like to go with the flow of popular sentiment rather than sit it out and hope it eventually died a natural death.

'Certainly not by me!' Polly lashed back at him, one small hand lifting in emphasis off the rail.

Without warning Rashad caught her hand in his, studying the slender bones below the skin that was so pale against his bronzed colouring and the intricate tracing of blue veins at her inner wrist. As if under a compulsion, he bent his proud head and pressed his mouth to that soft, smooth, delicate skin.

Polly studied that down-bent head in complete shock while tiny little tendrils of prickling awareness traversed her entire body. That one little contact was so screamingly sensual she couldn't believe it. She had had passionate kisses that left her cold as ice but the brush of Rashad's mouth across her wrist made her nipples tighten almost painfully inside her bra and forced a surge of hot liquid heat to rise between her thighs in a manner that made her rigid with discomfort. She quivered, shaken, aroused, suddenly out of her depth with him in a way she had never been before. When that skilled mouth roved across her palm and shifted to enclose a single fingertip and suck it, her knees trembled and her legs almost gave way beneath her in response.

Mesmerised, Polly looked up into shimmering golden eyes alight with raw sexual hunger.

An urgent burst of Arabic sounded from somewhere

behind them and she flinched in surprise while Rashad immediately dropped her hand.

Hakim was outraged by what he had seen. He had trusted his King. He had overlooked the reality that his King was a young man with all the appetites of a young man in the company of a beautiful young woman.

'This meeting is most improper,' Hakim informed his granddaughter unhappily. 'But I do not blame you for it.'

Further exchanges took place over Polly's head, which was bent because she was seriously embarrassed. After all, she had requested the private meeting and was guilty of disrespecting what appeared to be the cultural norms of Dharia. Rashad had only kissed her hand though, for goodness' sake, she thought angrily, thoroughly disliking the old man who had intervened and who was contriving to behave as though he had interrupted a raw and shocking sex scene.

'I am Hakim, Miss Dixon,' the older man informed her gently as he led her off the terrace. 'May I call you Polly? Or is it Zariyah?'

With difficulty, Polly recalled her manners. 'No, my grandmother wouldn't call me by my birth name. When I was old enough to understand it *was* my true name, she told me it was foreign and outlandish and she refused to use it, so she gave me the name Polly instead.'

'That is a great pity but perhaps in time that could be remedied,' Hakim remarked incomprehensibly above her head. 'Would you be willing to talk to me? I have something of very great importance to tell you…'

# CHAPTER FOUR

HAKIM ESCORTED HER to a room that he described as his office but which more closely resembled an old library.

Polly sank down in a comfortable armchair but sat bolt upright again, eyes wide with astonishment, when Hakim informed her that he was her grandfather.

'But how could you possibly know that?' she whispered unevenly.

'My mother…' Hakim handed her a creased old photo of a smiling blonde woman. 'My son, your father…'

Polly peered down in wonder at the photo of the attractive dark-eyed young man in the photograph. 'Is his name Zahir Basara?'

Hakim gently corrected her pronunciation and regretfully informed her of her father's death when the palace had been overrun twenty-odd years earlier. Tears stung Polly's eyes as he broke that news while frankly admitting that he and his only child had been at odds at the time of his demise.

'He wanted to marry your mother,' he explained. 'But I refused to support him. My own parents had a mixed marriage. My mother was the daughter of a

Swedish missionary working here. Although my parents stayed together they were not happy. My prejudice blinded me towards the woman my son loved—'

'I can understand that…but are you really sure that your son was my father? His is the name my mother left me with the ring, but—'

Tears dampened Polly's cheeks as her emotions spilled over because she felt so horribly guilty for doubting that name now. How much had she let her grandmother's bitterness colour her own attitude towards her mother? Annabel Dixon had not been lying, nor had she been unsure of who had fathered her first child. Her late mother had told her the truth.

'There can be no doubt because we did a DNA test. A sample was taken from you by the doctor without your permission,' Hakim confided gravely. 'DNA samples of the dead were conserved after the coup that killed our King's family and many others at the palace. I am very sorry that we ordered the test to be done without your awareness—'

'But why *did* you order it?' Polly murmured in bewilderment, too preoccupied by what he had told her to be angry when it had resulted in her finding an actual blood relative of her late father's. 'Why would you do such a thing?'

With quiet assurance, he explained that her arrival with both the Hope of Dharia ring and the name of a former queen had roused the suspicion that she could be a child of Rashad's late father. 'He was a most unscrupulous man with women. He had many extramarital relationships. We are not aware of any children born from those liaisons but it has always been a possibility. Imagine my astonishment when the computer found a match with my own son...'

Polly was just beginning to adapt to the shattering idea that she was in the company of her actual grandfather, who appeared to be a great deal more warm and pleasant in character than her maternal grandmother had proved to be. 'It must have been a nasty shock—'

'No, it was wonderful,' Hakim contradicted with a wide smile. 'My wife, your grandmother, wept with joy and cannot wait to meet you. We are strangers but we would dearly love to be considered family...'

At that generous statement, Polly's eyes flooded with tears again. 'I think I would like that too. Apart from my sister, I've never really had what people call a family. But doesn't it make a difference to you that Zahir and my mother weren't married?'

'But they *were* married,' her grandfather countered and he explained.

'My mother must've been devastated,' Polly commented sickly, trying to imagine the pure horror of marrying the man you loved and losing him again the next day.

'Dharia was in uproar and naturally Annabel fled home to the UK. There was nothing here for her to stay for. She must also have been aware that Zahir's family were hostile to her,' he completed sadly. 'I was very much in the wrong in the way I dealt with their relationship, Polly.'

A small hand covered his and squeezed comfortingly. 'You didn't know. You made a mistake. You wanted the best for your son. You didn't know what the future held...none of us do,' she pointed out quietly.

Hakim beamed at her, his rounded face flushed with pleasure. 'Will you give my wife and myself the opportunity to get to know you?' he asked humbly. 'We would be very grateful.'

Polly mumbled that she would be equally grateful. Tears were tripping her up again and she blinked them back in exasperation but her needle-in-a-haystack search for her father had come to an amazing conclusion. Her father was gone, as was her mother, but she had discovered other relatives to comfort her for that loss. It was more, she felt, than she could have hoped for before she set out on her journey.

'But do not be holding hands with the King again,' Hakim advised in an undertone. 'The fault was his, not yours, but I will not have your reputation soiled.'

'Are relations here in Dharia between single men and women so strict, then?'

'Only when the King is involved,' her grandfather admitted wryly. 'He is a public figure. He must not be seen to resemble his late father by practising any over-familiarity with a female. Once he is safely married, he will not need to be so concerned about appearances.'

Polly's right hand tingled and her face warmed while she distractedly recalled what Rashad had done with her finger. She wondered what an actual kiss would have felt like. With her imagination catching fire at the idea, a wanton charge of heat filtered through her lower limbs and filled her with self-loathing embarrassment. 'Is he planning to get married, then? Has he a wife lined up?'

'Not as yet but he *must* marry,' Hakim told her cheerfully. 'It is a monarch's duty to take a wife and have children to provide stability for the next generation.'

As far as Rashad was concerned, there was definitely a high price to be paid for all that bowing and scraping and luxurious privilege, Polly acknowledged ruefully. She remembered him saying that breaking the rules brought consequences and remembered how quickly Hakim's censure had brought those consequences home. Rashad had known exactly what he was talking about. She had been naïve and thoughtless, she reckoned ruefully, and, if Rashad was never allowed to be alone with a woman, surely it was little wonder that he had got a little carried away with her hand?

Wasn't it even possible that her request to see him alone had given him the wrong impression? Polly winced at the suspicion that he might have believed she was deliberately inviting that kind of attention. But on another level, warmth was still pooling in her pelvis at the recollection. He was a very handsome, very sexy guy and, for Polly, it had been an educational experience to finally realise why other people made such a fuss about the act of sex. If a man just kissing your hand could make you feel that overheated... At that point, she broke off her wandering thoughts and buried them deep.

Her maid wakened her with breakfast at what appeared to be dawn the next morning and told her with eyes that danced with mischief that she was going on a trip. Polly was not told where she was going or why or whose company she would be in and she assumed that that was probably because the young woman's small stock of English wasn't up to that challenge. She wondered if Rashad had managed to contrive some discreet way of returning her to her holiday plans but, when she began packing, the maid's confusion suggested that that was not the explanation. Had her kindly grandfather made some arrangement for her? Regardless, Polly was delighted by the prospect of seeing a little more of her father's country because all she had so far seen were the city streets and the view from the palace rooftop.

The maid led her down a service staircase and through a long tracery of quiet corridors and courtyards that suggested they were taking a more than usually circuitous route through the sprawling palace. They finally emerged into a garage packed with opulent vehicles and with noticeable ceremony she was ushered into an SUV. As they filtered out through the palace gates she noted that another two cars were accompanying them.

She would phone Ellie later, she promised herself guiltily. In truth she didn't want to hear any more of her sister's dire predictions after Rashad had bluntly explained the status quo. She didn't like the situation and neither did he, but there really wasn't very much that could be done about it, was there? It wasn't his fault or hers that his people had chosen to weave her into the legend of his great-grandmother and the fire-opal ring.

While the convoy of vehicles drove out into the desert, Polly settled back in the air-conditioned cool to enjoy her sightseeing. When they began to trundle up and down dunes, she told herself it was exciting although in reality the steep inclines and declines unnerved her. At one stage they passed by a long train of camels laden with goods and there was much hooting of car horns and shouted exchanges. When they descended the last dune she saw the oasis and her breath caught in her throat because that lush spread of green dotted by palm trees and a natural pool was so very beautiful and inviting in such an arid dusty landscape. The car came to a halt and the door was opened.

Without warning, Polly was engulfed in a whooping and chattering crowd of women. It unsettled her but the sociable smiles were a universal language of intent and she smiled as much as she could in response. That tolerance became a little more taxed when she was led into a tent and a long dress was presented to her with the evident hope that she would take off her trousers and tee shirt to put it on. Briefly, Polly froze while she wondered if trousers on a woman were a cultural no-no in such company and she decided to change for the sake of peace. Furthermore the dress, which was covered with blue embroidery, was really very pretty and she surrendered, not even objecting when her hair was unbraided and brushed out because it seemed to give her companions so much pleasure and satisfaction.

Ellie would tell her that she was much too busy being a people-pleaser to do as she liked but Polly loved to make those around her happy, she conceded guiltily as she was escorted between black capacious tents and taken into a very large one overlooking the pool. She sank down in the merciful shade and then Rashad strode in, as informally dressed in jeans and an open shirt as she was formally dressed.

'Rashad...' she murmured in sincere surprise, feeling her entire body heat as hot as the sun outside and her muscles pull taut in reaction to his sudden appearance. 'I suppose I shouldn't call you that. It's too familiar. What do—?'

'You call me Rashad,' he interposed without hesitation. 'How are you feeling after what Hakim told you last night?'

'Still shocked but mainly...' Polly considered thoughtfully '...incredibly happy to have discovered who I am even if I feel very sad that my father is no longer with us. I also like my grandfather.'

'He is a fine man, fiercely loyal and wise.' Rashad tilted his arrogant dark head to one side and lifted a broad shoulder and dropped it again in a sort of fluid fatalistic shrug that was as electrifyingly sexy as all his lithe physical movements. 'When he finds you gone from the palace this morning, however, he will be ready to kill me—'

'You arranged for me to be brought out here?' Polly frowned. 'Why?'

'It was bring you here or jump balconies to visit you in your bedroom. The bedroom would have been the worst option of all,' he told her with derisive amusement lancing through his stunning dark golden eyes.

In truth, very little amused Rashad in the sardonic and cynical mood he was in. He had spent most of the night thinking rather than sleeping, angrily confronting the issue that Polly's arrival with the ring had created and coming to terms with his own position. And the truth of what he should be doing had soon faced him. *There was no choice.* She was the woman his people wished him to marry. No other woman could even hope to fit into a legend. In reality he did not wish to marry at all but that was *his* problem, scarcely the problem of the people he ruled. His sense of duty, moreover, was strong. He would not be a selfish ruler like his father; he would put his people first and foremost in his life. It would be a challenge to remarry even though he could see decided advantages to marrying Polly, whom he, at least, *desired.* He believed that choosing an unknown wife from a photograph, basing the decision on her heritage and what others with a vested interest said about her, would be much more likely to lead to a dissatisfactory marriage. After all, at least he had got to *meet* Polly and draw his own conclusions…

Rashad's eyes were surrounded by the blackest, thickest, longest lashes she had ever seen on a man, Polly was acknowledging giddily, briefly wondering why every cutting edge in his lean dark features was set so hard, from his exotic cheekbones to his aggressive jawline, lending a tough, angry edge to his face. Assuming that that could only be a misapprehension on her part, she savoured the truth that he was still drop-dead beautiful in a way she had never known a man could be.

It was a serious challenge to drag her attention away from either his lean, darkly handsome features or his tall, powerfully muscled body. Indeed the sheer pull of Rashad's erotic allure thoroughly unsettled Polly because she could now feel and recognise the desire he incited in her and it was like nothing she had ever felt in her life before. That physical hunger that she had tried and failed to feel with other men was much more powerful and all-consuming than she had expected.

'I had you brought out here to the oasis so that I could ask you to marry me,' Rashad informed her levelly.

'But we're strangers!' Polly exclaimed in disbelief, totally unable to understand what he had just said and take it seriously.

'No, we are not. I already know much more about you than I would know about a bride I chose from a photograph…which, by the way, is my only other option,' Rashad admitted, choosing to tell her that unattractive truth. 'An arranged marriage would be considered normal for a man in my position although the practice has died out in our society. I've already had one arranged marriage and I don't want another—'

'You've already had *one*? You've been married before?' Polly whispered in wonderment, because she knew he was only thirty-one years old.

'I was married at sixteen—'

'I'm sorry but I think that's…barbaric,' she muttered helplessly. 'You were far too young—'

'We both were but those were more dangerous times and alliances had to be made and marriage was how it was done,' Rashad explained. 'I had no choice and I would very much prefer to have a choice this time.'

'But you said you felt *trapped* by your people's expectations,' Polly reminded him, dancing round the whole topic of his proposal rather than actually getting to grips with it because she just couldn't comprehend the enormity of what he was suggesting. 'Now you say you *want* to meet those expectations—'

'Why not? They chose you but I choose you too,' Rashad murmured huskily, his dark eyes flashing gold over her intent and expressive face. 'I want you.'

And his earthy appraisal left her in no doubt of what he was referring to. That hungry sensation surged and pulsed along her nerve endings and flipped her tummy over to leave her breathless. Her skin flushed, her body coming alive, and she shut her eyes because she could no longer withstand the intensity of his hot gaze.

'And you want me,' Rashad told her with maddening confidence.

Polly's eyes opened and her hands knotted into fists. 'I think you've—'

'No, don't fight me…it turns me on and if you do that I can't promise to keep my hands off you as I should,' Rashad framed in a roughened tone of warning.

'*It turns you on…*' Polly repeated in wonderment.

'Because nobody *ever* fights or argues with me. You can have no idea how boring that becomes,' Rashad admitted grimly.

In possession of a very sparky and forceful sister, Polly almost disagreed because she could not imagine finding pleasure in the apparently stimulating effect of dissension. Instead she said nothing, she simply shook her head. 'Sexual attraction is not a good basis for marriage—'

'It is for me,' Rashad countered without hesitation. 'I am convinced that you would make me the perfect wife.'

'But nobody's perfect!'

'More perfect than flawed,' Rashad qualified smoothly. 'The discovery that you have Dharian blood in your veins only adds to your appeal. This is your world now as much as it is mine and you have a family who will love and support you here.'

Polly bent her head down to escape the temptation of his glittering dark eyes. It was a powerful argument to know that there was another world and another family for her to explore. Apart from her sister she had never had a caring family to lean on, which was why Hakim's welcome had meant so much to her. She wanted to get to know that family and their culture, she wanted to spend time with them, which, with the cost of travel set against her low salary, would be very difficult once she returned home as scheduled at the end of the week.

'There would be advantages and disadvantages to marrying me,' Rashad outlined with dry practicality. 'I do not believe you would be unduly influenced by my wealth but as my wife you would be very rich. On the other hand, you would lose the freedom to do and say exactly as you wish because royals are expected to behave according to protocol. Sometimes that protocol feels stifling but it is there for our protection.'

Polly flushed very pink because although he had

said he hoped she would not be unduly influenced by his wealth, her mind had immediately flown to the good she could do with more money and she was mortified by that embarrassing moment of unwelcome self-truth. But poor Ellie was steeped in student debt and struggling and would be for many more years to come. Moreover, both sisters were desperately keen to trace their missing youngest sister, Penelope, and get to know her, but the hiring of a private detective was utterly beyond their financial means at present. She swallowed hard, ashamed of her thoughts and deciding that money had to be, in truth, the root of all evil and temptation.

'What happened to your first wife?' she asked him abruptly to escape those shameful thoughts of wealth and what she could do with it.

'Ferah contracted blood poisoning from a snake bite and died five years ago,' Rashad revealed in a harshened undertone. 'She did not receive medical attention quickly enough.'

'I'm sorry,' she murmured automatically because her mind was reeling under the burden of all that he had said and her own desperate confusion.

'Do you have an answer for me?' Rashad prompted with an air of expectancy on his lean, strong face.

'Not yet,' she admitted, matching his honesty.

Her brain had flatly rejected marrying him at first. They barely knew each other and it would be insane... *and yet*? She did want him, in fact she wanted him more than she had ever wanted any man and she was not an impressionable teenager any longer. In fact, what if she *never* met another man who made her feel the same way that Rashad did? That terrible fear held her still and turned her hollow inside because he made her feel alive and wanton and all sorts of things she had never felt before. And what was more, she was discovering that she *liked* the way he made her feel.

'Perhaps I can help you to make up your mind,' Rashad murmured with silken softness. 'You will see it as a form of blackmail but in reality it is the only possible alternative if you do not wish to marry me—'

Polly's head reared up, blue eyes wide and bright. 'Blackmail?' she exclaimed in dismay. 'What are you talking about?'

'If you don't marry me, you will have to leave Dharia immediately. Only your departure will end this madness on the streets and in the media.'

Polly was aghast at that cold-blooded conclusion. 'You're willing to throw me out of the country?'

Hard dark eyes held hers. 'If that is what it takes, yes…and naturally I would not wish you to return in the near future,' he decreed harshly.

Polly was shaken by that solution because she had been planning to get to know her grandparents, her newly discovered Dharian family. She had no doubt that Hakim and his wife would be willing to visit her at least once in London but it would not be the same as staying on in Dharia and having the chance to explore her father's heritage and culture for herself.

'I cannot allow the current security situation to continue,' Rashad informed her grimly and he went to the doorway of the tent to clap his hands. 'We will have tea while you consider your options.'

Polly didn't see how tea was going to be the answer to anything but the sheer amount of entertaining ritual involved in the brewing of tea by two robed men at least gave her something to watch while her brain struggled to deal with a rising tide of anxiety. He was using blackmail even if on one level she could understand his position. It was very unfair from her point of view, though, that she should have to suffer for something that was in no way her fault. In many ways by piling on that extra pressure of an immediate departure, he was taking her right to choose away from her.

'Seriously...' she began furiously, 'you would actually force me to go home?'

'When it comes to what is best for my country I will always do it,' Rashad countered with a roughened edge to his dark deep drawl. 'That is my duty.'

Polly compressed her taut lips, her hand clenching angrily round her cup. She knew he meant it. It was stamped in the resolve that had hardened his lean, darkly handsome face. Either she stayed on in Dharia and agreed to marry him or she went home again and stayed there. She didn't need to be pregnant to be offered a shotgun marriage, she reflected angrily. That was what he was offering her with the crowds providing the firepower of pressure.

Yet when it came to marriage all that went with Rashad in terms of baggage and culture and his people's expectations was simply huge. Even so, she quite understood why he was willing when his next-best option was a marriage to a complete stranger about whom he would essentially know nothing.

'Of course, you'd get the ring back if you married me,' she said with a flat lack of humour.

'And gain a gorgeous blonde wife,' Rashad traded with a sudden charismatic smile that lit up his bronzed face, illuminating the hard cheekbones and hollows that gave his features such strong definition.

Polly glanced across the fire pit at him and the knowledge that if she said no she would never see him again sliced into her like the sudden slash of a knife blade. That prospect, she registered in mortification, was not something she wanted to think about. No more easily could she imagine being forced to walk away from the new family she had found. Perspiration beaded her upper lip as she fretted.

Marrying Rashad would be like taking a huge blind leap in the dark and she wasn't the sort of woman who took risks of that nature, was she? But if it worked, there would be much to gain, she reasoned ruefully. She would have her grandparents for support. She was already powerfully attracted by Rashad.

'The answer is…yes. It's insane but…*yes*,' Polly muttered almost feverishly before she could lose her nerve.

Although relief slivered through Rashad at her agreement that relief was threaded with undeniable resentment over his predicament. After all, he had been backed into a corner and forced to marry again. This was *his* choice, he reminded himself sternly. *She* was his choice and far superior to a bride who would have been a complete stranger, but the stubborn streak of volatility Rashad always kept suppressed had flickered from a spark into a sudden burning flame, for it was impossible for him to forget how very much he had hated being married.

# CHAPTER FIVE

'IT'S NOT TOO late to change your mind,' Ellie said with
a hint of desperation while she watched the television
to see the partying taking place in the streets of Kashan
to celebrate Rashad and Polly's wedding day. 'Well,
they probably do have you on the tea towels and you
would need to be smuggled out of the country in dis-
guise if you *jilted* him!'

'Obviously, I'm not going to jilt him,' Polly said
quietly, wishing her sister would stop winding up her
nerves with her dire forecasts.

Ellie had landed in Dharia forty-eight hours earlier
and she had given her elder sister every conceivable
lecture against marriage since her arrival.

*Marry in haste, repent at leisure. Do you realise
what you're getting into? Are you even sure you will be
his only wife? What if everything Rashad shows you on
the surface is simply a front to persuade you to marry
him? Look at those people partying at the announcement! He needs you more than you need him. That
should make you suspicious. What if he has another
woman hidden somewhere? A woman he really loves?*

Polly had dutifully listened to every possible argument but she had absorbed few of her sibling's warnings for the simple reason that she suspected that she was falling in love with Rashad. Yes, she had finally worked that out all on her own. How else had she contrived to overlook his threat to throw her out of the country if she didn't agree to marry him?

On her side of the fence, her reasons for marrying Rashad had become resolutely practical over the two short weeks that had passed since his proposal. One, her grandfather spoke very highly of his ruler, and she trusted Hakim and his wife Dursa because she was genuinely convinced that they would rate her need for happiness higher than any desire to see their grandchild wed their King. Two, Rashad had been honest with her. He had paid her no extravagant compliments and had made no mention of love and she had accepted that latter handicap with the strength of a patient, optimistic woman because she hoped that in time his feelings for her would change. Three, there was just something very powerful about Rashad that called to Polly on a very deep level and she couldn't put it into words or explain it, so she had come to think of it as the start of love. She simply knew that she wasn't capable of walking away from him.

And how did she know that? she asked herself as the cluster of chattering maids surrounding her twitched at the skirts of her elaborate wedding outfit and attached more jewellery to her, although she was already laden down with gold and precious gems because Rashad's uncle had saved the family jewel collection along with his youngest nephew. How the fire-opal ring had become detached from that collection would probably never be known but Hakim believed that his son had very possibly taken it and given it to Polly's mother, Annabel, for safekeeping during the chaos following the explosion that had claimed the lives of Rashad's family. Her father, Zahir, had after all been the most senior soldier in the palace that awful day and had died himself within twenty-four hours.

She could never walk away from Rashad when her own family was so deeply involved with the country of Dharia. No, she knew that even if her marriage turned out to be a bad marriage she was very likely stuck with it until the day she died because her grandfather had spelt out to her that she had to think in terms of for ever when it came to marrying a ruling king. Rashad's father had divorced twice before wedding Rashad's mother and those matrimonial breakdowns had been interpreted as signs of his general instability and his lack of staying power and sense of duty as a monarch.

'And even worse, you've hardly seen Rashad since you agreed to marry him,' Ellie reminded her with anxious green eyes.

'He's had so many people to meet and so many arrangements to make,' Polly responded quietly, for Rashad had spent the last fortnight travelling around Dharia. 'He has to consult with others about everything he does to come up with a consensus. It's the way he operates to keep everybody happy that they've had their say and Grandad says it works beautifully.'

Ellie stood back a step to examine her sister's gorgeous appearance. Traditional red and gold embroidery and rich blues had been laid down on the finest cream silk fabric that flowed like liquid and screamed designer just like the matching shoes. Her head was bare, her hair loose, as was the norm in Dharia for a bride. A magnificent set of sapphires glittered at her ears, her throat, her neck and her wrists. Delicate henna swirls decorated her hands and her feet and beneath the dress she wore a chemise with a hundred buttons for her groom to undo on the wedding night. Ellie was more intimidated than she wanted to admit by the pomp and ceremony of Rashad and Polly's wedding and the deep fear that she was losing her sister to another world and another family. She knew that Polly's affections ran loyal and true but how could she possibly compete?

As for Rashad? Well, it went without saying that he was very, very nice to look at, very well spoken as well as educated and civilised but, like the buttons waiting to be undone beneath Polly's dress, what was her future brother-in-law *really* like below the smooth polished façade? That was the main source of Ellie's concern because in her one brief meeting with Rashad she had reckoned that a great deal more went on below that smooth surface than trusting, caring Polly was probably willing to recognise. A man traumatised as a boy by the loss of his entire family, forced into marriage at sixteen, widowed ten years later and then raised to a throne over a population who worshipped him like a god because he had rescued them from a dictator's tyranny? That was quite a challenging life curve to have survived. How much did her sister genuinely know about the man she had agreed to marry?

'Would you *please* stop worrying about me?' Polly urged Ellie with troubled blue eyes. 'I want this to be a happy day.'

'I'm always happy if you're happy,' Ellie declared, giving her a gentle but fond hug of apology.

But Polly knew different. Ellie had always been a worrier, expecting the worst outcome in most situations. She refused to borrow that outlook, wanting to look forward with all the hope and optimism that her wonderful discovery of her loving grandparents had already fanned into enthusiasm. Why shouldn't their marriage work out? She wasn't expecting an easy ride. Of course there would be obstacles and surprises and disappointments but surely there would also be joys and unexpected benefits along the way?

She refused to admit even to her sister how isolated and rejected she had felt at having barely spent even a moment with Rashad since agreeing to marry him. And worse still and far too private for her to share, how very apprehensive she actually felt at the prospect of having sex for the first time with a man she had yet to even kiss...

The wedding was to be very much a public event and screened on television. Refusing to give way to nerves, Polly went downstairs with her sister and her bevy of chattering companions to be ushered into the throne room that had been set up to stage the ceremony.

A sharp pang of regret pierced her that she should still have an unknown sister who could not be part of her day and she wondered how soon after their marriage it would be acceptable for her to ask Rashad for his financial help with that problem. How else was she to locate their missing sister, Penelope?

As she strove to ignore the camera lenses while at the same time studiously trying not to do anything unsightly with her face, her nervous tension surged to an all-time high. And then she saw Rashad, exotically garbed in magnificent red and gold ceremonial robes, and all her anxiety was swallowed alive by a sense of awe and wonder that she was on the very brink of marrying such a divinely handsome male. She felt ridiculously schoolgirlish when she looked at him but, on another, much more intimate level, she also felt surprisingly wanton.

Rashad made her wonder about stuff that she had truly never wasted time thinking about before because for so long sex had been part of other people's lives but never hers. That was just how it had been while her freedom was restricted by her grandmother's long illness. Her gaze locked onto the wide sensual curve of Rashad's mouth and she simply tingled as she wondered what he would taste like, what that glorious long bronzed muscular physique of his would look like naked and, inevitably, what it would be like to be in bed with him. As her colour fluctuated wildly, a tide of heat claimed her innermost depths to encourage an embarrassing dampness at the heart of her and she pressed her thighs together and stood rigid as a rod to discourage her colourful imagination. It embarrassed her to be so very impressionable.

'Wow…' Ellie mumbled at her elbow, overpowered by the sheer medieval splendour of their surroundings. 'Who's that guy with the bridegroom?'

'Some Italian Rashad went to uni with. I haven't met him but I think his name is Rio,' Polly whispered, unable to focus on anyone but Rashad because she was now wondering why her future husband looked so impossibly moody and tense. Didn't he realise that he should be smiling for the cameras? Or was any show of human emotion forbidden to him as a ruler? Or was it even possible that he genuinely loathed figuring as a leading light in such a public event?

The ceremony was short and sweet, translated into both their languages. Polly's hand trembled in the firm hold of Rashad's when he slid the ring onto her slender ring finger. His slightest touch invoked a storm of churning, rippling awareness throughout her entire body and she was embarrassed by it, questioning that it could be normal to be so susceptible to a man. But that anxiety was squashed by her astonishment when she belatedly registered that her wedding ring was a feminised miniature of the famous fire-opal ring that Rashad wore on his hand. It seemed deeply symbolic to Polly that he had deliberately made a feature of the ring that had first brought them together and a brilliantly warm and happy smile softened her previously tense mouth as she looked up at him with starry eyes of appreciation.

His wide sensual lips almost made it into an answering smile of acknowledgement but his shimmering dark eyes remained cool and evasive and a faint pang of disappointment touched Polly. Yet somehow she sensed that his self-discipline was so inflexible and so intrinsic to his character that he would not allow any relaxation of his innate reserve to betray his true feelings. Simultaneously and for the very first time she wondered what those feelings actually were...

Of course she knew and accepted that he wasn't in love with her, even respected his essentially honest nature because he had not tried to deceive her with any false show or foolish promises. But there was something so distinct about his obvious emotional withdrawal that she felt guiltily unnerved by it.

At least Polly was pleased about the ring, Rashad was thinking wryly. It was very probably the first *positive* thought he had had in the two frantic weeks of meetings and reorganisation required before it was possible for him to free up the time to become a husband. And future father, he reflected joylessly. Back to the life of being a sperm donor and praying that the seed took root this time around, he reflected with a pang of distaste. That was, after all, he believed, the *only* reason for him to even get married: to father a child and create the generational continuity for the throne that his people needed to feel safe in the future. He recalled Ferah's heartbreak when she had learned that she had a medical condition that made conception a virtual impossibility and guilt engulfed him over his derisive musings. The ability to have a child would have meant the world to his first wife.

Did Polly have any idea what she had got herself into? And why hadn't he made the effort to warn her?

Why hadn't he? he asked himself afresh, disconcerted by that truth and belatedly recognising that he could have told Polly many things that would have put her off marrying him but that, inexplicably, he had shared not a single one of them. He breathed in slow and deep, more than a little disturbed by the worrying nature of his failure to discuss something so very crucial to the likely success of their marriage. His conscience was suddenly laden down by that awareness.

Admittedly it was a sore subject from his point of view and he saw no good reason to dangerously overshadow the present with the tragic clouds of the past. In truth he had never shared his feelings about marriage with any living person and loyalty and honour demanded that he protect his first wife's memory. After all, Ferah had suffered horribly from the stigma of a ten-year childless marriage and in death she deserved his respect at the very least.

'You need to smile,' Polly whispered under her breath as Rashad guided her out of the throne room in front of an audience of clapping and cheering well-wishers.

'Why?' he whispered back, long-lashed dark golden eyes narrowed. 'It is a solemn occasion.'

'But you're behaving as though you're at a funeral,' Polly muttered in instinctive complaint while they took their seats at a massive long top table in a giant banqueting room already filled with tables.

No, not a funeral but possibly the bonfire of his most

unrealistic hopes, Rashad labelled cynically, his facial muscles tightening so that his bronzed skin traced his sculpted features even more closely. He had hoped to stave off marriage for at least another few months but Polly's explosive effect on the Dharian population had killed that possibility in its tracks. But now that he had fallen dutifully into line, hopefully everybody would be happy for a while and he could relax again. With another person beside him though, with a *wife*... His lean, darkly handsome face tensed again, his dark eyes flashing gold with disquiet until he looked at her afresh. His very beautiful wife, who had shivered with excitement when he'd kissed her hand. He almost groaned at how hard that tantalising memory made him.

As the reception wore on Polly became increasingly troubled by Rashad's grave demeanour. For a split second she glimpsed Ellie laughing uproariously at the side of Rashad's friend, Rio, and that stark contrast sobered her even more. Surely the bride and groom should appear even happier? But Rashad wasn't talking, he wasn't smiling, he was the very antithesis of happy and she was shocked and unnerved by it. Most particularly, Ellie's warnings were haunting her again.

*How much do you really know about Rashad?*

And all of a sudden Polly was in the deeply unenviable position of admitting that she knew virtually nothing about the man she had just married. As soon as the meal was done she submersed herself in her grandparents' sincere happiness on her behalf and their evident conviction that she had married a man who would move heaven and earth to make her happy. Seemingly they saw nothing amiss with Rashad's behaviour.

Was he one of those very moody men one heard about? Oh, dear...oh, no, she thought in dismay at the prospect of being wed to a man who switched from sun to shade at the roll of a dice. Or was it only her that was noticing—or *imagining*—that something was wrong? Was she seeing Rashad from a different perspective now? After all, Hakim was very much a man who served his King and as long as Rashad was courteous her grandfather would be content with the surface show and question no deeper. But it was a little more complicated for a wife, Polly reasoned anxiously, particularly a wife, who suddenly felt as though she had married a stranger...or a Jekyll and Hyde character.

A white open-topped limousine, accompanied by a heavy escort, drove them slowly through the streets of the capital city to the airport. Hundreds of soldiers and police held the excited crowds back behind barriers. Polly waved and smiled as her grandfather had told her she must while marvelling that Rashad's marriage could ignite such demonstrations of sheer joy. She could only hope that she would somehow manage to live up to the people's no doubt high expectations of her and in an undertone, above the loud clamour, she shared that thought with Rashad.

'Get pregnant. That's probably the only thing they really want,' Rashad pronounced very drily.

Polly's blue eyes widened to their fullest extent as her head whipped round to stare at his lean, darkly handsome face in shock. 'Are you serious?' she framed, shrinking not just from his blunt words but from the harshness with which he voiced them.

'You can't be that naïve,' Rashad responded drily. 'It's not as though either of us have a choice in that department and that cliché about honeymoon babies would be a real feat to pull off.'

Polly had paled, the delicate lines of her face freezing as she carefully turned her head away again to dutifully continue waving and smiling. But neither the wave nor the smile came as freely or as easily as earlier because her heart had frozen inside her and her tummy had turned over sickly at his response.

When Rashad had said, 'I want you' was that why? He simply needed a wife to impregnate as quickly as possible? And why, oh, why was she only now thinking about something that should have been obvious to her from the outset? Obviously a king wanted and needed an heir. She hadn't even thought about birth control and now she could see that even the mention of it would go down like a lead balloon. Was she ready to get immediately pregnant? Were they to have no time to become accustomed to living together as a couple before they became a family?

Rashad noticed that Polly had transformed into a still little statue by his side and faint dark colour flared along his cheekbones because he was discomfited by the reality that he had taken his bitterness out on her. 'I'm sorry,' he said instantly. 'I didn't mean that quite the way it sounded.'

As if from a distance, Polly looked down at the lean brown hand suddenly resting warmly on hers but it was too little, too late from a bridegroom who had avoided all physical contact throughout the long and exhausting day they had shared.

Freeing her hand without making a drama of doing so, she said flatly, for the sake of peace, 'I'm sure you didn't.'

*I'm sure you didn't mean to be that blunt and insensitive.*

*I'm sure you didn't mean to make me feel like a rent-a-womb.*

*I'm sure you didn't mean to pile so much pressure on me when conception is not something I can control.*

*I'm sure you didn't mean me to see just how ruthlessly pragmatic you are about conception.*

*But you did.*

She kept up her valiant smile but her eyes stung with tears and her heart felt as if he had taken it in his hand and crushed it. What remained of her determination to have a happy wedding day drained away as well.

If he wasn't prepared to make any effort, why should she?

# CHAPTER SIX

POLLY DROPPED OFF into a nap on the helicopter flight. The noise of the engine combined with her fatigue to simply knock her out. She surfaced when Rashad shook her shoulder. Flushed and bewildered, briefly not even aware of *where* she was, she stumbled stiffly upright to move to the exit, only to be scooped out and carried away from the craft like a bundle. But the natural heat of Rashad's body penetrated even through their clothing and she stiffened in dismay, engulfed by the glorious scent of him. It was a typical Eastern layered fragrance and the already familiar hints of sandalwood, saffron and spice were outrageously exotic and she breathed him in dizzily, all her senses firing as he settled her firmly into the vehicle awaiting them.

'Where are we?' she framed slightly unsteadily when Rashad climbed in after her.

'By the sea. My grandfather used to come here to fish,' Rashad proffered, sounding rather more animated than he had earlier.

And in reality, he was feeling much more relaxed than he had been at the outset of the day. Haunted as he was by destructive memories, the wedding had been like a long dark tunnel of recollection he'd had to fight his way through without betraying himself. But then he would feast his gaze on his bride and the wild seething hunger she incited would claim his brain like an intoxicating drug that made rational thought impossible.

In the midst of recalling their last conversation, Polly stiffened and glanced at him from beneath her eyelashes in a quick sidewise foray, noting the classic purity of his strong profile and the more relaxed line of his beautiful mouth. Evidently escaping the wedding fervour at the palace and the street celebrations in Kashan had revitalised him.

'When I was a little boy, my grandfather brought me here to stay with him several times,' he told her.

'So, you're into fishing?' Polly gathered, forcing herself to speak, to make the effort, although it was hard when she herself was in a remarkably tough and unforgiving mood. He had spoiled her day. He had ridden roughshod over her feelings. But then maybe Rashad didn't have much in the way of feelings, she reflected, feeling downright nasty because he had hurt her. Get knocked up on the honeymoon and please everyone? He had very much picked the wrong bride for that little project. And yet that brief instant when he had carried her out of the helicopter had enveloped her in a cascade of erotic anticipation that made her want to lock herself away because she wasn't quite sure she could trust herself to maintain restraint around him.

'No, I'm not,' Rashad admitted. 'Fishing is too slow a pastime for me. I only have such good memories of those trips because it was rare for me to receive any male attention in those days. I literally never saw my father…and for that matter, I seldom saw my mother. I was my father's third son by his third marriage and of very little importance in the royal household.'

'So, there was a sort of hierarchy in your family?' she remarked, her curiosity engaged in spite of her mood. She was taken aback to learn that he had had little contact with his royal parents even before their death. Yes, she had grasped that her mother had been his nanny but she had still possibly naively assumed that he had continued to enjoy regular interaction with his mother and father.

'Of course. Nobody ever said no to my eldest half-brother because they believed that one day he would be King. Naturally as third in line behind two healthy siblings it was not considered possible that I would ever inherit the Dharian throne.'

Polly watched his lips part and then close again, his strong jaw clenching. She knew that he was remembering the two half-brothers who had died with his parents and her soft heart was pierced on his behalf. 'I'm sorry that you had to lose your family to become what you are today.'

'As God wills,' he murmured with husky finality.

Night was folding in fast around them. The sun was going down in scarlet splendour over the dark shimmering sea while against that backdrop and raised on a rocky outcrop above the beach she could see the silhouette of a battlemented stone building. 'A…castle…?' Polly mumbled. 'We're going to stay in a castle?'

'My grandfather and his friends once used it as a fishing lodge. Don't worry,' Rashad told her, misinterpreting her reaction. 'It's not as medieval as it looks. Our private apartments were renovated soon after I became King. The castle is one of our national treasures—'

'You mean it's open to the public?' she prompted in surprise.

'Only when we're not using it—which means it's open most of the year. It's a Crusader castle and if we want to attract tourists we must offer historic sites. The royal family owns all the sites but from now on we will share them with our people.'

Minutes later, Polly slid out of the car in a stone courtyard while staff rushed around them bowing and grabbing up luggage and smiling endlessly to display their pleasure at their arrival. And Polly thought in wonderment, Rashad's *talking* again. Was that because it was their wedding night with all the expectations that that signified? What else could it be? Her chin lifted and her mouth compressed.

They were ushered into a giant stone room furnished like a very opulent historical set piece. She gazed in awe at the huge scarlet and gold fabric-draped four-poster bed and the matching silver and mother-of-pearl-inlaid furniture. 'Please tell me there are modern washing facilities somewhere,' she whispered.

With a husky laugh, Rashad opened a small arched door in one corner and spread it wide to display the marble-tiled bathroom, presumably custom built to fit the circular turret room.

His laugh and that spontaneous smile brought her head up again, silvery blonde hair spilling across her shoulders, and she connected with black-lashed golden eyes so heated in their steady regard that something in her pelvis burned, liquefied and positively ached. Her heart raced and her face hurt with the effort it took not to smile back but how could she smile and forgive and forget when all her husband wanted her for was to provide him with an heir? He had pretty much ignored her throughout their wedding day, she reminded herself stubbornly, and if his outlook had improved it could only be because he now expected to have sex with her.

Momentarily, as she freshened up at the vanity unit, she paused when she caught a glimpse of her hectically flushed face in the mirror. She couldn't do it— she *couldn't* do the sex thing coldly, on demand, not the way she felt now!

She had always wanted that first experience to be special and she had expected it to be special with Rashad right up until he had made her feel like an anonymous female body to be impregnated. Was she being unfair? Even unreasonable? She knew he needed an heir but following on from his behaviour throughout their wedding that had been a step too far into the dark for her to accept.

Her body was hers alone to share or deny. She had always been the least likely woman to be coaxed into doing anything she didn't want to do because for all her eagerness to please she had always had a very strong sense of self. But until she met Rashad she hadn't actually *wanted* to have sex with anyone, not that acting as her grandmother's carer for years had given her many opportunities in that department, she conceded ruefully. But right now, this night, *this* moment felt very wrong to her because she needed more from Rashad than he had so far given her to feel safe with him…and yet?

Deep down inside she wanted him, *craved* him as much as her next breath of air, she acknowledged in driven discomfiture. Her brain might say one thing but her body was singing an entirely different tune. Her breasts were full and tight and there was something like a little flame burning low in her pelvis that had made her all tender and damp and aching in a place she had literally never thought about before. But it wasn't right, she reminded herself doggedly. Where was her self-respect? Her courage?

*Well, what are you waiting for?* she asked her now wildly flushed reflection in the mirror. She had to tell him before expectations got out of control.

Rashad watched Polly emerge from the turret room and he strode forward, involuntarily drawn by the sheer effect of her delicate ethereal looks and all that beautiful trailing white-blonde hair. He stretched out a hand to clasp her smaller one, tugging her to him with an impatience he couldn't control even though his brain was warning him to go slow. There was so much hunger inside him for the bubbling warmth of her smile and the as yet undiscovered delights of her slender body and he wrapped his arms round her to capture her.

'Rashad…' Polly gasped, disconcerted by that sudden advance.

'You're my wife now. In some ways, I don't really believe it yet,' he confided in a thickened undertone, slowly winding a brown hand into the fall of her silky hair, long brown fingers gently caressing her pale-skinned throat. 'I can't believe you're mine—'

'Yes, b-but...' Polly stammered, struggling to hold onto her wits that close to Rashad when she could feel the thump of his heartbeat through their clothing and the heat and strength of his big muscular body against hers. He was fully aroused and she could feel the hard thrust of him against her. In receipt of that very sexual message the kind of brutal need she had never had cause to feel before held her rigid with momentary indecision. In that instant she wanted *so* badly to let him touch her just as she urgently wished to touch him. She ached to smooth explorative fingers over that long bronzed muscular body and learn everything that had until now been denied her.

'And there is no fancy protocol that can keep us apart now,' Rashad continued with a raw-edged smile of satisfaction, his gorgeous black-lashed, dark golden eyes locked to her wide blue gaze as he lowered his head.

His sensual mouth came down on hers with a devastating hunger that travelled through her slight length as violently as a lightning bolt. His tongue plunged deep, electrifying her with sexual desire. He tasted so good she moaned into his mouth, helpless in the grip of her desire to deny herself, never mind him. Rashad pushed up the long trailing length of her dress and found her, fingers flirting with the silky panties she wore and then sliding beneath the elastic to find her feminine core. Something similar to spontaneous combustion detonated at the heart of Polly's quivering body. She was so eager to be touched, she felt scarily out of control and that shocked her, reminding her that she *had* to pull back if she was to have any hope of defusing a difficult situation with honesty. Feeling as she did, it was wrong to be submerging herself in wholly physical sensation, she reminded herself fiercely, and she yanked herself back out of his arms with so much force that she stumbled back against the footboard of the huge bed, her hair tumbling across her face.

Taken aback by that vehement withdrawal, Rashad stayed where he was, a bemused frown forming between his black brows, dark yet bright as stars eyes glittering and narrowing. He had never looked more beautiful to her disconcerted gaze. 'What's wrong?' he asked levelly.

'I can't do this with you tonight,' Polly muttered hoarsely, still struggling to control the inner quaking of need that had momentarily burned right through her defences. Even as she stood there she was alarmingly aware of the pained ache between her thighs, the high of her excitement abating with painful slowness. 'I'm sorry, I can't. I'm not ready to go to bed with you… er…yet…'

'We are married.' Rashad framed the words with pronounced care, without inflexion, without expression. 'We are man and wife. What possible objection could you have?'

'Probably nothing that you will really understand,'

Polly countered in a discomfited tone. 'I hardly know you, Rashad. I haven't really even seen you since I agreed to marry you and today you were weird—'

His extreme stillness remained eerily unchanged. 'Weird?' he repeated darkly. 'In what way?'

'How can you ask me that when you wouldn't speak to me or look at me or even touch me if you could avoid it throughout the wedding festivities?' Polly demanded emotionally. 'I would have settled for friendliness if that was the best you could do.'

'Polly…it was a state wedding with television cameras and an army of onlookers. *Friendly?*' An ebony brow elevated in apparent wonderment and his entire attitude made her feel small and stupid and childish. 'I don't have the acting ability to relax to that extent in that kind of public display—'

Polly had turned very pale. 'It was more than that. You acted like…like you were *hating* having to marry me!'

Rashad lost colour below his bronzed skin, his strong facial bones tightening, because in truth he was in deep shock at what was unfolding. He was a very private man. Even as a child he had been forced by circumstance to keep his thoughts and feelings absolutely to himself. And in all his life nobody had ever been able to read him as accurately as *she* just had and it made him feel exposed as the fraud he sometimes feared that he was. He had done his duty, he conceded bitterly, but clearly he had not done it well enough to convince his bride. 'Why would you think such a thing of me?'

'If you lie to me now, it will be the last straw!' Polly warned him shakily. 'I deserve the truth.'

Rashad angled his proud dark head back in the smouldering silence that had engulfed them. Somewhere in the background Polly could hear the timeless surge of the sea hitting the shore outside and, inside her own body, she could feel the quickened apprehensive beat of her heart.

'For me, the last straw would be that you have married me today and now, quite independent of any reason or discussion, have decided that you will *refuse* to consummate our marriage!' he bit out rawly. 'That, by any standards, is unacceptable.'

His roughened intonation made Polly flinch at the standoff she had hoped to avoid by explaining her feelings. 'Trust a man to bring it all down to sex!' she shot back bitterly. 'Of course you can't get me pregnant if we don't have sex, so I suppose that has to be your main grounds for complaint—'

'I've had enough of this,' Rashad ground out abruptly, too many damaging memories tearing at him to allow him the calm and patience required to deal with an emotionally distraught bride. 'I'm going out.'

Polly was stunned by the idea that he would simply walk out on a row. 'You can't just walk out... Where are you going to go, for goodness' sake? We're on a beach surrounded by desert in the middle of nowhere! And what will people *think*?' she exclaimed in sudden consternation.

'Let me see...' Rashad inclined his handsome dark head to one side in a way that made her want to

slap him, the slashing derision in his gaze unhidden.
'They will think that a honeymoon baby is unlikely,'
he breathed curtly. 'But thankfully they will not know
that my bride refused me!'

He strode through a connecting door she hadn't noticed until that precise moment and the door thudded
shut in his wake. The silence that spread around Polly
then felt claustrophobic and, her throat tight and dry,
she collapsed down on the side of the bed, her lower
limbs limp as noodles. What had she done? she asked
herself in belated consternation. What on earth had she
done? The right thing? Or the *wrong* thing?

In the room next door, Rashad paced the floor,
smouldering with a rage so emotionally powerful it
disturbed even him. But he never ever lost his temper
with anyone because the need to regulate any potentially dangerous outburst had been beaten into him
at an early age. He had taught himself to master his
volatile nature, he had taught himself to quell the passion that fired him and…and walk away. But the look
on his bride's face when he'd walked away had been
frankly incredulous. Too late he was discovering the
downside to marrying a woman unafraid to fight and
argue with him.

As he paced, on several occasions he strode back
towards the door that separated their rooms, eager to
defend himself, but each time he stopped himself and
backed off again. What, after all, *could* he say to her?
That the knowledge he was on show in front of cameras invariably paralysed him with unease? That such
intense attention had never been welcome to him and

that her ability to behave with cool normality had astounded him? A man, particularly a king, was supposed to be stronger than that, more disciplined, more able to perform the essential duty of public appearances. A king was not supposed to be introspective or emotional, he was supposed to be a powerful figurehead, a flawless role model and a very strong leader. While Rashad reiterated his stringent uncle's most frequent directives inside his own head, he continued to pace in raging frustration.

He had married a foreigner with a different set of values. A foreigner who had fired an erotic hunger in him that was stronger than anything he had ever expected or even *wanted* to feel. In such a situation, it was downright unnerving and absolutely outrageous to positively *crave* another opportunity to argue with her. Tearing his attention from the door between them, he ripped off his ceremonial robes and donned more comfortable clothing. He had stayed long enough out of view not to rouse household comment at his abandonment of his new bride, he reasoned grimly as he left the room and strode down to the stables.

At least his horse wasn't going to ask him unanswerable questions and pick up on his deficiencies, he reflected with bitter humour. He wasn't sure of his ground with Polly, he acknowledged, furious at that demeaning reality. In truth his previous experience with Western women had been purely sexual and casual and nothing more than that. But he did have considerable experience of being denied sex. That Polly should do that to him when he recognised that she felt the same chemistry he did had enraged and frustrated him beyond bearing.

What did she want from him? What the hell did she expect from him? So, he had acted *weird*?

Possibly a bit stiff and silent, he interpreted as he directed his stallion, Raza, across the desert sands at a pace that his guards were stretched to match. But then Rashad had been born to the saddle and raised from the age of six within a nomadic tribe, who ranged freely across the vast desert landscape that spanned several countries and recognised no boundaries. That same innate yearning for complete freedom had been bred into his bones but the sleeker, more sophisticated man he had inevitably become wished he had paused to take a cold, invigorating shower before his departure.

He didn't get women, he reflected, recalling Rio once admitting the very same thing. And if Rio, an incurable playboy with vast experience of the opposite sex, didn't understand women, how was Rashad ever to understand the woman he had married?

Ironically he had been brought up to believe that he would own his wife's body and soul much as he owned his horse. Maybe he should've thrown that at her to show how far he had travelled from the narrow-minded indoctrination of his youth. So backward had his ancestors been that they would have taken such a refusal as a justification for forcing the issue. He was fairly certain Polly would not have been impressed by that admission and he could not imagine ever wanting to physically hurt a woman. But there were other ways of harming and hurting a wife. Even by the tender age of six he had heard and seen enough in the palace of his childhood to grasp that his mother was pitied by some and blamed by others for his father's relentless debauchery. That was why when Polly had banished him from the marital bed he had wanted to protect her reputation by waiting in the room next door.

But, in spite of that concession, Rashad remained blazingly, scorchingly angry with his bride. What a way to embark on a new marriage! This was not what *he* had wanted. Separation was not a way forward and sex was not a reward for good behaviour. And what was Polly's idea of good behaviour? Rashad hadn't a clue. He was right back to where he had started out, utterly in the dark as to what way he had somehow contrived to fall short…

Eventually, and only once Polly had surrendered all hope that Rashad would reappear and discuss their quarrel, she removed her jewellery and undressed and got into the giant bed. She felt curiously overwhelmed and deflated by the reality that she was *alone* on her wedding night. She couldn't even understand her own reaction, because she had *asked* him to leave her alone and now to feel dissatisfied on that score seemed perverse.

In truth, she recognised ruefully, on some level inside herself she had expected Rashad to reason, persuade or even seduce her into changing her mind. But Rashad hadn't done anything so predictable. Instead he had walked out on her. Angry? Bemused? Hurt? She discovered that she didn't like to think that he was either hurt or confused by her behaviour. But she *must* have hurt his pride, she finally acknowledged unhappily, wondering why she had not foreseen that very obvious consequence.

The next morning, she came awake with the sunlight. At some stage while she still slept her luggage had been unpacked. Her grandparents had insisted on equipping her with a new and more appropriate wardrobe to wear after the wedding. She had picked out styles she liked with a trio of Dharian designers and had been concerned by the likely cost of such exclusivity even after Hakim assured her that he was well able to afford such a generous gesture.

Polly extracted a comfortable dress and smilingly dismissed the maid kneeling at the door ready to assist her into her clothing. The blue sundress was light and airy and, with canvas shoes on her feet, she sat down to breakfast on the terrace on the floor below, to enjoy the view of the sea while telling herself repeatedly that she was not one whit bothered by Rashad's vanishing act. At some stage of the night that had passed, however, she *had* reached new conclusions about what she had done.

When she had been getting so wound up before the wedding, Rashad had been completely absent and unable to answer or soothe any of her concerns. Her sister's dire fear that she was making a mistake had encouraged her own insecurities, which in turn had exploded when Rashad had appeared to act differently throughout their wedding day. Had she imagined that he was different? Had she been looking for trouble, seeking a fatal flaw that would give her the excuse to step back and take stock of her new marriage? After all, what did she want from Rashad when she already knew that he didn't love her?

Honesty, respect, trust, caring, affection, she listed anxiously, her lovely face clouding as she acknowledged the unrealistic level of desired perfection inherent in making such a list about a man, particularly on the very first day of a brand-new marriage.

When Rashad in person appeared out of seemingly nowhere and joined her without fanfare and with a seemingly relaxed smile to bid her a good morning, Polly was so disconcerted she almost fell off her chair in shock.

'My goodness, I was wondering where you were!' she exclaimed helplessly.

Her attention involuntarily welded to the impressive physique outlined by a white tee shirt that hugged his muscular chest and biceps and faded jeans that outlined his narrow waist and long powerful thighs. In fact, although the sun hadn't at so early an hour been bothering her, she heated up so much she began to perspire. 'Last night—'

'We will not discuss last night,' Rashad broke in decisively. 'We were both overtired after the wedding.'

'Seriously…we're sweeping the dust under the carpet?' Polly muttered in astonishment.

Rashad answered her in Arabic, and then with an affirmative yes, the sculpted full line of his eloquent mouth firming, his devastating dark eyes cloaked by his lashes.

A fair brow lifted in growing disbelief. 'And you think that's *all right*?'

'I think it is better than the alternative,' Rashad told her truthfully, heaping sugar into his mint tea.

Polly stared down blindly at her own tea. 'What happened to the man who said dissension could be stimulating?'

'He learned that that brand of stimulation can be treacherous,' Rashad countered with level cool.

And that fast, Polly wanted to scream at him again and so powerful was that urge that her teeth chattered together behind her murderously compressed lips. He could set off a seething emotional chain reaction inside her and make her madder than anyone else had ever done and it seriously unsettled her. She sipped at her tea with a stiff-fingered hold on the tiny glass cup and looked out to sea in angry silence, her mouth tightly compressed.

'You see now we have nothing to talk about because you can't gloss over a major row and simply pretend it never happened,' she then pointed out, not feeling the smallest bit generous, especially not after having lain awake for half of the night wondering where he was, how he felt and what he was doing. Evidently if he simply moved on past the dissension without requiring any contribution from her, he had done no such wondering.

'We did not have a row, we had different opinions.' Rashad persisted in his peace-keeping mission much as he persisted against all odds to direct challenging meetings staged between enemies and rivals.

Polly almost lunged across the table as she leant abruptly forward, silvery blonde hair rolling across her slim shoulders like a swathe of heavy silk. 'I *want* a row!'

Rashad levelled resolute dark eyes on her, raw tension gripping him because he only had to look at that rosy soft mouth of hers to want to back her down on the nearest horizontal surface. Hell, it didn't even have to be horizontal, he acknowledged, his inventive mind rushing to supply every erotic possibility imaginable. His jeans uncomfortably tight around the groin, he flexed his broad shoulders. 'You're not getting one.'

'Even if I say please?' Polly pressed helplessly, because she genuinely believed that they had to discuss what had happened to move beyond it.

'With regret…not even if you beg,' Rashad spelt out a tinge more harshly. 'Rows are divisive and risky and we will not have them—'

'Says the King. But we still need to clear the air,' she muttered, shaken by an increasing fear that he really did believe such an approach could work.

'As far as I am concerned the air is already clear and further discussion would be overkill,' Rashad concluded in a tone of finality as he began to peel a piece of fruit, waving away the manservant who immediately approached him in a keen attempt to save him from the labour of such a petty task.

'Well, then you can *listen*,' Polly told him in desperation.

Rashad tensed at that seemingly new threat, dark eyes flashing gold below lush black velvet lashes as he focused on her. Why was she trying to destroy his calm and enrage him again? He had behaved honourably the night before. He had not argued. He had not threatened. He had walked away. This morning he had not uttered one word of reproach. If he had told her how he *really* felt about what she had done his anger would've blown the roof of the castle off and scared her. Whether he liked it or not, he was what he was, the heir to a ruthless lineage, and his belief that his wife belonged to him ran like a thread of steel through his every reaction even while his intelligence told him that life didn't work like that any more.

She looked so innocent and so very beautiful and yet she was totally off-the-wall crazy in Rio's parlance, Rashad acknowledged ruefully. Yet why did he continue to find that strange trait so incredibly attractive? Why, when he was in the worst possible mood, did that trait make him want to smile? He concentrated on his tea, which was less likely to unnerve him than the odd thoughts assailing him without warning. He told himself that he didn't want to listen, didn't want further criticism or a greater burden of guilt. After all, he knew who was ultimately at fault. Somehow he had screwed up. If his brand-new bride wasn't happy, he had to be to blame.

'And perhaps now that you've eaten you could dismiss the staff?' she added in a disturbing indication that she was likely to become loudly vocal once again.

Rashad signalled the two hovering servants to dismiss them before springing upright with fluid agility and sitting back down on the low wall bounding the castle ramparts.

Polly immediately froze in her seat. 'No, don't do that,' she said anxiously, blue eyes fixed to him in dismay.

'Don't do...*what*?'

'Don't sit there with your back turned to a dangerous drop,' Polly urged.

Rashad studied her in disbelief and then glanced round in a sudden movement that made her gasp to scrutinise the dangerous drop she had complained about. A couple of hundred feet of scrub and rocks sloped gently down towards the beach and he had climbed it many times with a blindfold as a little boy on a dare.

'Please get up and move away from it,' Polly whispered unsteadily.

Rashad studied her again, noticing how pale and stiff she had become. 'It's *not* a dangerous drop—'

'Well, it is to me because I'm terrified of heights and just looking at you sitting there is making me feel sick!' Polly launched at him at vastly raised volume with only a hint of a frightened squeak, her annoyance at his obstinacy having risen higher still.

Rashad raised calming hands as though he were dealing with a fractious child and rose with exaggerated care to move to the castle wall. OK...point taken.'

Polly flushed to the roots of her hair and slowly breathed again. 'I just don't like heights—'

'I think I've got that,' Rashad confided straight-faced.

'So, you're planning to listen now to me?' Polly enquired stiffly.

Impatience flashed through Rashad and no small amount of frustration at her persistence. Water dripping on stone had a lot in common with his new wife. But he was clever enough to know that listening was an important skill in negotiation and experienced enough to know that marriage encompassed an endless string of compromises and negotiations. 'I'll listen but not here. I'll show you round the castle and you can talk… quietly,' he added softly, but the dark-eyed imperious appraisal that accompanied it was a visual demand for that audible level. 'No shouting, no crying, no dramatic gestures.'

'I don't do crying and dramatic gestures,' Polly told him in exasperation.

By nature, Rashad recognised the ironic fact that, of the two of them, *he* was more volatile and more likely to be dramatic and his handsome mouth quirked at that sardonic acknowledgement. The night before, Polly had been very understated but a rejection was a rejection, no matter how it was delivered, and not a pattern Rashad wanted to find in his wife. He looked at her; in truth he never tired of looking at her and the plea in her shadowed blue eyes would have softened the heart of a killer.

'OK,' he agreed grudgingly. 'But if you embark on another argument—'

'You'll lock me up and throw away the key,' Polly joked.

'Considering that that is exactly what my ancestors

did with their wives, you could be walking a dangerous line with that invitation,' Rashad murmured, teasing on the surface but fleetingly appalled by how much that concept attracted him when it came to the woman smiling back at him.

# CHAPTER SEVEN

'EVERYTHING HERE IS unfamiliar to me. Your lifestyle, the customs, the language,' Polly murmured quietly as they walked along the battlements past stationed guards to take advantage of the aerial views. 'When you add you and a new marriage into that, it can occasionally be overwhelming.'

That made remarkably good sense to Rashad, who had been braced to receive a quiet emotional outpouring of regrets and accusations. Relief rising uppermost, he squared his broad shoulders and breathed in deep. 'I can understand that.'

'And I've barely seen you since the day I agreed to marry you. I realise that with your schedule you had no choice but it made me feel insecure.'

Rashad was downright impressed by what he was hearing, it never having occurred to him that a woman in a relationship with him could speak her mind so plainly and unemotionally. In silence he jerked his chin in acknowledgement of the second point.

'Yesterday was a very challenging day for both of us.' Polly's voice shook a little when Rashad settled an arm to her back to steady her on the uneven stones beneath their feet, long fingers spreading against her spine to send a ridiculous little frisson of physical awareness travelling through her all too susceptible body.

'It was…'

'I've never been in a serious relationship before…'

Rashad stopped dead. *'Never?'* he questioned in disbelief. 'But you are twenty-five years old.'

Polly explained about her grandmother's long, slow decline into full-blown dementia and the heavy cost that had extracted from her freedom while her sister was away at university. 'So, if I'm a little inexperienced in relationships, you'll have to make allowances on that score,' she told him tautly.

A frown line was slowly building between Rashad's ebony brows. His fingers smoothed lightly up and down her spine as if to encourage her to keep on talking as he stared down at the top of her pale blonde head, far more engaged in what she was telling him than she would have believed.

Polly could feel the heat of embarrassment rising into her cheeks in a wave. Gooseflesh was forming on her arms, the hairs at the back of her neck prickling while the warm hand at her spine had tensed and stilled. 'And I think that may be why I sort of freaked out last night because I was a bit nervous…*of course* I was…and you hadn't made me feel safe or special or anything really!' Conscious her voice was rising in spite of her efforts to control it, Polly looked up at Rashad in dismay and discomfiture.

And for the very first time, Rashad understood his bride without words and he felt like the biggest idiot ever born because he had been guilty of making sweeping assumptions without any grounds on which to do so. It had not once crossed his mind that Polly might be less experienced than he was. Indeed he had even worried just a little that he might not be adventurous enough or sophisticated enough to please her. With a sidewise glance at the guards studiously staring out at the desert and the beach, Rashad bent down, scooped his surprised bride up into his arms and carried her indoors. Doors were helpfully wrenched open ahead of him by the staff as he strode back to their bedroom.

'What on earth are you doing?' Polly exclaimed when he had finally tumbled her down in a heap on the giant bed in which she had slept alone the night before.

'Giving us privacy,' Rashad advanced with a sudden smile of amusement that sent her heart racing. 'I don't wish to offend you but I had made the assumption that you would have enjoyed at least a few lovers before me—'

'And why the heck would you assume that?' Polly demanded with spirit.

'Your values are more liberal. Here, although young adults now tend to choose their own partners, it is still the norm for women to be virgins when they marry. That would be more unusual in your society.'

'I suppose so,' Polly conceded reluctantly because she knew her sister fell into the same 'unusual' category, Ellie having admitted that she had yet to meet a man who could tempt her into wanting to cross that sexual boundary. 'But my sister and I were both brought up in a very strict home. My grandmother believed that both I and Ellie were illegitimate and until she fell ill she policed our every move because she was afraid that we would repeat what she saw as our mother's mistakes and come home pregnant and unmarried.'

'I know very little about your background.' Rashad settled fluidly down on the edge of the bed in a relaxed movement. 'Even your grandfather warned me against having unrealistic expectations of you—'

Polly flushed scarlet. 'My...*grandfather*? Please tell me you're joking—'

'There was no discussion, Polly, but I guessed what he meant. He merely wished to protect you from the risk of me being naïve in that line. I am *not* naïve,' Rashad completed with wry emphasis. 'But Hakim and I have naturally never discussed anything that intimate, so he could have formed no idea of my attitude in advance.'

In receipt of that explanation, her mortification ebbed. It was evident that her grandparents had made the same assumption and she couldn't find it in her heart to fault her grandfather for trying to shield her from the threat of Rashad's disappointment.

'You're not that old-fashioned,' she commented with a helpless little giggle. 'But obviously Grandad is.'

'I spent several years studying at Oxford University and that was an enlightening experience being a mature student,' he told her wryly.

'Must've been,' Polly conceded, picturing Rashad with his film-star good looks and wealth let loose to enjoy a student's freedom. 'Was that after your wife passed away?'

His lean, strong face tensed. 'Of course. I could not have left her behind here to be oppressed by her father.'

Polly frowned. 'How…*oppressed*?'

'In essence my late uncle was a good man but he was also a bully. I say that with respect because without his intervention I would not be alive,' Rashad admitted levelly. 'On several occasions during Arak's dictatorship rumours of my continuing existence put a price on my head. I could have been hunted down and killed like an animal but the tribe took me in as one of their own and protected me because my uncle was their sheikh.'

It was the first time he had given her a little window into the sheer turmoil of his formative years and it sobered Polly as nothing else could have done. Certainly it could not have been all rainbows and roses being brought up by a bully, most particularly not if he owed his very life to that same bully, who had coolly married the putative future King of Dharia off to his own daughter at the age of sixteen. Her heart was touched and she pressed her hand briefly against a lean masculine thigh in silent empathy.

'It seems we do, in spite of all that has happened, have something in common,' Rashad remarked with a flashing smile of such intense charisma that she couldn't drag her attention from his lean, darkly handsome features. 'We were both raised by strict guardians.'

'Yes,' Polly conceded feverishly, encountering the dark golden depths of his eyes with a mouth that was running dry and a stomach awash with butterflies as awareness of their proximity kicked in with electrifying effect.

'I do not want you to be nervous of me, *habibti*,' Rashad confided huskily. 'I promise you that I will never do anything that you do not want.'

'I…I pretty much want everything!' Polly confided with a strangled little laugh of self-consciousness because she didn't feel it was fair to go on acting as if she were a terrified virgin because she was not.

'*Everything…*' Rashad savoured the word and she flushed. 'I love your honesty.'

And he kissed her, slowly, carefully, nibbling at her lower lip, then tracing it with the tip of his tongue. In fact he turned up the temperature so gradually she was barely aware that one of her hands had crept up to spear into his thick black hair and the other to tighten on a strong shoulder. She wanted more, much more, she acknowledged, her whole body turning warm and languorous in response while the little prickles and tingles of desire were already pinching at her nipples and warming her pelvis.

'I will make it special,' Rashad intoned into the scented depths of her tumbling hair, his dark deep drawl roughened by the knowledge that she was giving him her trust.

'You can't promise that,' Polly felt forced to tell him prosaically. 'If it hurts, it's not your fault. I'm not *that* ignorant—'

'Hush…' Rashad groaned.

'No, you stop setting standards,' Polly warned him

playfully, tracing his hard jawline with a gentle fore-finger, marvelling at how much closer she felt to him as he pressed her back against the pillows and leant back to flip off her shoes, letting them fall to the tiled floor.

'I've done that all my life—'

'But not here, *now*…when it's only the two of us,' Polly persisted helplessly.

And for a split second, Rashad contemplated the strangeness of not seeing everything in the light of passing or failing and shouldering the blame, but it was too engrained a habit for him to even imagine. He shook off that alien concept and homed in on his bride instead, studying that ripe rosebud mouth with an amount of hunger that threatened his control.

He kissed her again and the passion he couldn't con-ceal burned in that kiss and it thrilled her as much as the hungry thrust of his tongue melding with her own. He was *so* intense, she thought tenderly, no mat-ter how hard he tried to hide it. He took far too many things far too seriously. Maybe she would be able to make him lighten up a little and relax more. But that solemn thought was quickly engulfed by the intoxi-cating delight of his demanding mouth crushing hers beneath his own. Little noises she didn't recognise es-caped her throat.

He slid her out of her dress with admirable ease, so deft at the challenge that she was a little surprised to find herself lying there clad only in her lace underwear. All of a sudden she was worried about what he would think of her body, which she knew was kind of aver-age. Breasts neither large nor small but somewhere in between. Hips a little larger than she would have liked, legs and ankles reasonably shapely, she reflected ruefully, shutting her eyes, just lying there, not wanting to beat herself up with such foolish thoughts.

'*Ant jamilat jiddaan*… You are so beautiful,' Rashad told her with fervour, and she dared to open her eyes again.

And yes, it *was* her body he was scrutinising much as if she were the seventh wonder of the world. Emboldened, Polly arched her spine to make the most of her assets, relishing his admiration while thinking no more about her physical imperfections. Her blue eyes settled on him and she murmured shyly but with determination, 'You're still wearing too many clothes.'

His dark golden eyes gleamed with appreciation and he pulled off his tee shirt to reveal a bronzed and indented muscular torso worthy of a centrefold. The tip of her tongue crept out to moisten her dry lips as her gaze crept inexorably down to the revealing bulge at his groin. Apprehension was the last thing on her mind as he unzipped his jeans, showing her the intriguing little dark furrow of hair snaking down over his taut flat stomach. She stopped breathing altogether as he came back to her and fastened his mouth hungrily to hers again, the warmth of his big body against her an unexpected source of pleasure.

He unclasped her bra and cupped a pale pouting breast, long fingers toying with the taut pink tip, rolling it, gently squeezing the distended bud before sucking it into his mouth and teaching her that that part of her body was much more sensitive than she would ever have believed. The tug of his lips on the straining tips of her breasts sent a pulling sensation arrowing down into the heat rising between her thighs. Lying still became a challenge while her hips dug into the mattress beneath her. The hollowed ache at the heart of her increased, making her restless and stoking her craving for more.

'You're not letting me touch you,' Polly muttered in a rush, gripped by the fear that she wasn't being much of an equal partner. 'Isn't this supposed to be a two-way thing?'

'It is but it would please me most if this first time between us is for you, not for me,' Rashad countered with assurance.

A little red in the cheeks, Polly abandoned her objections, particularly when he made a point of pinning her flat with another passionate driving kiss and her temperature rocketed up the scale. He tugged off her panties and finally touched her where she most longed to be touched, tracing the delicate skin at the apex of her thighs and concentrating on the tiny nub that seemed to control her every nerve ending.

The pleasure was the most irresistible sensation she had ever known. In an impatient movement Rashad disposed of his jeans and glided down the bed to part her trembling legs. She felt like a sacrifice spread out before him and it heightened her arousal. Before very long he contrived to teach her that what she deemed to be irresistible pleasure could grow exponentially to an almost unbearable level. And she had never felt her body rage out of her control before until those frantic feverish moments when Rashad thoroughly controlled her with his carnal mouth and skilful fingers. Almost immediately he transformed her keen curiosity into an overpowering demanding need. Her spine arched, her hips rose and jerked and her heart thumped as madly as though she were sprinting. And then stars detonated behind her eyelids and the whole world went into free fall along with her body.

He slid over her and ran his mouth down the sensitive slope of her neck to her shoulder. A compulsive little shiver racked her languorous length. Her lashes lifted on his lean, darkly handsome features and she smiled, a little giddily, a little shyly, recalling how much noise she had made in climax and the way she had clawed at his hair and his shoulders. He brought out the bad girl hiding inside her and she rather thought she liked that, and the shimmering gold satisfaction in his eyes suggested that he did as well.

He nudged against her tender cleft and she tensed, feeling him there, hard and ready. He pushed into her with greater ease than she had expected but then he had prepared her well. Her delicate inner walls stretched to accommodate him and then he shifted his hips and sank deeper, sending a sharp little pang of pain through her that made her grit her teeth.

'Do you want me to stop?' Rashad asked thickly.

'No…' she wailed in shocked protest as in answer to his movement an exquisite little shimmy of internal friction eddied through her pelvis.

Rashad was fighting to stay in control, struggling to think about anything other than what he was doing. He shifted again, gathering her legs up over his arms, and drove into her hard and fast, rewarded by the gasp of pleasure she emitted. She was very vocal and he loved her lack of inhibition. He gripped her hips and pounded into the hot, wet grip of her glorious body with a growl of savage pleasure.

Polly could only compare the experience to a wild and thrilling roller-coaster ride. A tightening band of tension formed low in her body and the crazy rush of intense sensation heightened as he quickened his pace, changing angle, hammering into her receptive body with delicious confident force. Excitement flooded her as another climax beckoned and she could feel her body surging up to reach it, gloriously out of her control. She hit that peak with a wondering cry and then dropped her head back against the pillows, drained but wonderfully relaxed. Rashad groaned and shuddered and buried his face in her tangled hair.

'That was amazing,' she told him cheerfully as soon as she had enough breath to speak, one hand smoothing possessively over his long, sweat-dampened back.

Rashad's dark head reared up, a startled look in his dark eyes as he searched her flushed and smiling face. And then he threw back his head and laughed. 'Polly… only you would tell me that!' he said appreciatively, dropping a kiss on her brow. 'I thank you. It was even more amazing for me, *aziz*.'

'Do you think it would have been like this for us last night?' she asked, suffering a belated attack of regret.

'No, we were both too tired and irritable and I had no idea I would be your first lover,' Rashad replied, letting her off that hook with newly learned generosity as he freed her from his weight and rolled over.

Her hand sought and found his below the sheet. Had she had the energy she would have turned cartwheels because she felt happy and too laid-back to guard her words. Succumbing to her curiosity, she said lightly, 'Your first marriage was arranged, wasn't it?'

His fingers flexed and tensed beneath the light cover of hers. 'Yes.'

'Did you love her?' Polly pressed helplessly, desperate to know even though she didn't understand why she should have such a craving to know that information.

'Yes,' Rashad replied, stifling his unease at being forced to think back to his miserably unhappy first marriage. 'How could I not? We were childhood playmates.'

And somewhere within Polly a little hurt sensation sprang up like a claw that had the power to scratch her deep where it didn't show. She didn't understand it because it was surely good news that he had contrived to love Ferah, regardless of the reality that it had been an arranged marriage. But perhaps she had not been quite prepared to hear that he had known Ferah so well, a young woman who would have understood so much more about Rashad than Polly probably ever would. Her predecessor, she acknowledged unhappily, would be a tough act to follow.

## CHAPTER EIGHT

'YOU'RE DOING VERY WELL,' Rashad assured Polly seven weeks later. 'Your posture is much improved.'

With the ease of practice, Polly ignored the audience of grooms and guards gathered round the palace horse paddock. When Rashad had first informed her that he planned to teach her to ride she had laughed out loud in disbelief and outright denial of the idea because Polly had never been into anything even remotely athletic. Unfortunately, Rashad considered the ability to ride a horse an essential skill and from the instant she was put aboard a four-legged monster and then panicked at the height she was from the ground, the lessons had begun. If you had a weakness, you worked hard to conquer it: that was how Rashad expected her to operate. And backsliding and excuses weren't allowed.

If Rashad knew the actual meaning of the word 'honeymoon' he was hiding the fact very well, Polly conceded with rueful amusement while her mount trotted obediently round the paddock, her own body moving easily now in the saddle as Rashad had taught her to move. When she had pleaded her fear of falling as an excuse to avoid the activity, Rashad had borrowed a mechanical horse from somewhere and set it up with crash mats in the basement gym and she had spent two ghastly days learning how to fall as safely as possible. At no stage had she required Dr Wasem's attention but she had certainly picked up a few bruises before she'd learned the technique of tucking in her arms and her head and rolling to lessen the impact of a fall. When the doctor had cautiously suggested to Rashad that learning to ride could be considered a rather risky activity for a woman hoping to conceive, Rashad had scoffed.

'That will probably take at least a year to achieve!' Rashad had remarked dismissively to Polly, releasing her from the fear that her ability to conceive would be under constant scrutiny.

In fact, on that score, she had worried unnecessarily, she conceded with relief. Rashad appeared to have neither a sense of urgency nor indeed any level of expectation when it came to the question of his bride falling pregnant. Of course they weren't taking any precautions either, so she supposed that over time the odds of conception would naturally increase. It could hardly have escaped her notice that his first marriage had been childless but, when taxed on that question, Rashad had quietly admitted that Ferah had had a medical condition that made her infertile.

Rashad lifted Polly down off the mare and stared down at her with brilliant dark eyes of satisfaction. 'I'm really proud of you,' he admitted huskily. 'You've conquered your fear.'

Polly grinned. 'I'm going for a shower,' she told him cheerfully.

Their audience had vanished back to their duties when she trudged into the building at the rear of the stables that housed luxury changing and washing facilities. They had stayed at the castle by the sea for only two weeks before Rashad's necessary attendance at an important meeting of his council had interrupted their seclusion. They had returned to the palace, where it was much easier for Rashad to oversee the progress of various projects and still take time off.

But Polly still retained tantalising memories of the sea and the castle. They had picnicked on the beach and gone swimming, for both of them were proficient in the water. They had talked late into the night on the terrace and rumpled the bed sheets until dawn lit the skies. By the end of that stay at the castle Polly had admitted to herself that she had fallen head over heels in love with her husband. He could charm her with a smile and seduce her with the smallest touch but his greatest skill was that he made her feel wonderfully happy and content.

Rashad had reached the shower block ahead of her. She started in surprise when she saw him: a lithe, dark, electrifyingly sexy figure sheathed in a polo shirt, tight riding breeches and riding boots. As soon as she appeared he shut the door and locked it behind her, towering over her as she relaxed languorously back against the stone wall. He ran a calloused fingertip lightly over her pouting pink lips and breathed thickly. 'I can't keep my hands off you when I think of you getting naked in the shower, *aziz*.'

A shiver of excitement as stimulating as a storm warning snaked through Polly's slender body. While formal in so many other ways, Rashad was wonderfully earthy about sex. Over the past weeks they had probably had sex virtually everywhere they were left alone together in the palace. In his office, in the stables, in unoccupied rooms he showed her round and once, thrillingly, over the dining-room table. Polly was equally challenged to keep her hands off Rashad's gloriously masculine body. And as many of their unplanned encounters had proved to be the most sensational she literally stopped breathing when a certain smouldering look appeared in Rashad's dark golden eyes. It made her feel like the most seductive and beautiful woman in the world. And it was a level of intimacy with a man that she had never dreamt of experiencing.

Polly leant back against the wall, almost boneless with anticipation of his touch, her blue eyes starry. She was intensely aware of her own body, already screaming a welcome as her gaze slid down his body to the desire outlined by his breeches and impossible to hide.

'Getting naked, Your Highness,' she murmured playfully, 'would appear to be a sensible idea.'

Rashad planted his hands beside her head and pushed his lean strong body into hers, letting her feel the urgency of his need. 'Sensible is the very last thing you make me feel—'

Polly gazed up at him, loving every proud line and hollow of his lean, hard face and the stunning black-fringed dark eyes that often made her breath hitch in her dry throat. 'Well, if I have to suffer, why shouldn't you?' she teased.

Challenged, Rashad dug his hands into the silky swathe of hair she had unbraided and brought his mouth crashing down in hungry demand on hers. The very taste of her was an aphrodisiac. He was wound up tight as a spring and Polly was the only woman who had ever had that much power over him. He craved her body like a drug and revelled unashamedly in her responsiveness. At first, his extreme need for her had disturbed him and he had tried to restrain that need, but a willing Polly in his bed every night, and most unforgettably a Polly wantonly bending over the dining-room table while offering him a cheeky smile of challenge, had demolished his resistance entirely. They had a scorchingly sexual and satisfying connection he had never thought to find in marriage.

Polly's clothes came off long before they made it into the shower. He tormented her swollen nipples with his mouth while his lean fingers probed the receptive wetness between her thighs and expertly fuelled her hunger. He hauled her up to him and brought her down on him, bracing her hips against the wall to take her with hard, forceful thrusts that made her cry out in excitement and blissful pleasure. Barely able to stand in the aftermath, she rested up against him for support and let him carry her into the shower.

'How useful are you finding Hayat?' he asked curiously as he switched on the multi-jets of water.

'She's indispensable,' Polly admitted, for she was

making her first official appearance as Rashad's wife that evening at a diplomatic dinner in the capital, Kashan. 'She's explaining everything I need to know. She's like a walking book on faces, etiquette, clothes. I couldn't do without her.'

'That's good,' Rashad responded, hiding his surprise at the news. Polly's grandfather had suggested Hayat for the role of supporting Polly and it seemed the older man must also have seen a side to the waspish brunette that Rashad had failed to appreciate. At the same time, however, as his sister-in-law, he acknowledged that Hayat deserved superior status and recognition.

Having shampooed her hair, Polly surveyed Rashad as he lounged back against the tiled wall, slumberous and relaxed and all male to her appreciative gaze. She padded forward and rested her hands down on his wide shoulders before slowly tracing them down over his washboard abs, watching his lush black lashes shift upward, his dark golden eyes shimmer tawny with renewed desire.

'You are so predictable,' she scolded. 'Do you ever say no?'

At that sally, Rashad grinned with unabashed enjoyment, slashing cheekbones taut below his bronzed skin. 'Do you want me to?'

And no, she didn't, she acknowledged as her hands went travelling down over his lean, powerful physique in confident reacquaintance. She turned him on and she liked that power very much, adored the way he closed his eyes and simply let her do as she liked with him, the evidence of his arousal hard and smooth and pulsing between her fingers. She stroked, cupped, knelt at his bare brown feet and used her mouth on him until he groaned and shuddered and lifted her up to him with impatient hands and brought her down on him again with all the explosive demanding passion he couldn't control. Afterwards she was limp with satiation and drowsy as he washed her down, showering away the proof of their intimacy and roughly rubbing her dry with fleecy towels. Having to get dressed again was a trial, she reflected.

'I'm so sleepy,' she complained as he walked her back through the palace, his hand engulfing hers and maintaining a physical link with her that she appreciated.

'Take a nap before this evening. You'll be standing around a lot meeting people before the meal,' he warned.

'Do you need a nap?' his bride asked him winsomely.

'We will neither of us sleep if I join you in our bed, *habibti*,' Rashad parried with highly amused dark eyes and a flashing smile of acknowledgement. 'I'll catch up on some work in my office until it's time to get ready for the dinner.'

Screening a yawn and wondering why she was so very tired when she slept like a log most nights, Polly stripped in their bedroom. She pulled on a nightie rather than shock her maid, who seemed to think that sleeping in the nude was scandalous, and she slid into bed. Her sore breasts ached beneath the fabric and she put her hands over them, momentarily questioning why she was getting all the usual symptoms of her period arriving but nothing was actually happening.

She was wakened with a light snack and tea and warned that Hayat was waiting to see her. Hayat was in charge of her wardrobe and her itinerary. Reluctant to keep the other woman waiting, Polly ate and dressed in haste to join her. As she pulled on her jeans and teetered on one leg a wave of giddiness attacked her and she lurched and fell back against the bed. Her maid started forward in dismay while Polly waved her back and breathed in slow and deep, remaining where she was until the sensation ebbed. Maybe she should've eaten a little more after so much physical activity, she thought ruefully.

'Nabila said you were unwell,' Hayat commented, moving forward. 'Should I call Dr Wasem?'

'A spot of dizziness, nothing more,' Polly dismissed, knowing that the smallest hint of illness was sufficient to send the whole household into a state of either panic or premature celebration on her behalf and, as she was well aware that it was simply 'that time of the month' when she never felt that great, she didn't want to cause a fuss. Hayat had educated her about the Dharian attitude to her health and Rashad's, admitting that concern on their behalf was easily awakened by rumour and speculation and generally overexcitable in nature. Rashad's bout of tonsillitis the year before had had the leading newspaper questioning why their King had not been hospitalised and had accused the royal household of risking his health with an old-fashioned hands-off approach to medicine. Dr Wasem had been mortally offended.

'You are sure you are feeling all right?' Hayat prompted. 'Your devoted husband would never forgive me if anything happened to you.'

'I'm fine,' Polly said, wondering why that word, 'devoted', had seemed to acquire a sarcastic edge on Hayat's lips. 'It's just that time of the month, that's all. I always feel a little run-down.'

The brunette gave her a tiny smile. 'I am sorry your hopes have been disappointed...'

Polly bent her head and rolled her eyes. Hayat and the rest of the household might be eagerly awaiting the announcement that she was pregnant but neither Polly nor Rashad were concerned, both of them believing that at the very least actually conceiving would take several months. Moreover such close scrutiny on such a score was seriously embarrassing. 'I'm not disappointed, Hayat. We're only newly married.'

'I watched my sister break her heart over her inability to conceive,' Hayat told her. 'It is very hard for a woman to be in that situation—'

'But I'm not in *that* situation,' Polly broke in, hoping to shut down the too personal conversation for, while she found Hayat very efficient, she maintained careful boundaries with her and never quite relaxed in her company. The brunette was unpopular with the other staff and Polly had taken heed of that warning to stay on her guard.

'Soon enough, as time goes on, you will be,' Hayat

forecast with a look of exaggerated sympathy on her pretty face. 'How could you not be concerned?'

Polly shrugged a stiff shoulder in dismissal of the topic. 'You wanted to see me?' she prompted, keen to push the conversation in a less personal direction.

'Oh, yes. I brought the royal jewellery for you to choose from,' Hayat pointed out, indicating the large wooden box on the table. 'But I left the amber set out for you because it will exactly match the dress you're wearing.'

Polly studied the very ornate gold and amber collaret and suspected her neck might break under the sheer weight of it. 'It looks very heavy—'

'It's a favourite of Rashad's. The set first belonged to his mother,' Hayat told her quietly.

Hayat was a fund of such information about Rashad and the royal family and Polly invariably took the brunette's advice. Well, if Rashad liked it… she thought ruefully, although she was challenged to imagine him even noticing what she was wearing. He wasn't that kind of man. He didn't notice much in the way of feminine detail, having once tried to describe a dress she'd worn and he'd admired as 'that blue drapey thing'.

When it came to more practical matters, however, Rashad was a roaring success, she thought fondly. She loved Rashad so much more than she had ever thought she could love any man and, while as yet he might not love her, he was definitely attached to her. In a crowded room, his attention continually sought her out. Her favourite British foods now magically made regular appearances at mealtimes. Flowers arrived for her every day. Furthermore, he had insisted that they should settle Ellie's student loans, Polly thought with pleasure as she went into the bedroom to phone her sister in privacy.

'Ellie is part of *our* family now,' Rashad had pointed out. 'In the same way as your other sister will be when we eventually find her.'

Rashad had hired a London investigation agency to search for her missing sister the very day after she told him about her existence. Indeed Rashad took on Polly's deepest concerns as if they were his own and she loved that trait because for the first time ever she felt cared for and looked after without being made to feel like a burden or a nuisance. In the dark of the night she wakened to find him wrapped round her and, even though she got far too hot sleeping that close to him, she rejoiced in their closeness and kicked off the bedding instead of pushing him away.

'Polly!' Ellie exclaimed with satisfaction. 'I've got news about Penelope.'

'Oh, my goodness,' Polly muttered in shock, dropping down on the edge of the bed.

'Don't get too excited,' Ellie warned her. 'We haven't found our sibling yet but that investigation agency Rashad's London lawyer suggested certainly seem to know what they're doing—'

'Money talks,' Polly said wryly.

'Don't I just know it.' Ellie sighed guiltily. 'Here I am free of all my student debt thanks to the two of you.

I can't ever thank you enough for that. I've got all sorts of choices now that I didn't have before—'

'Penelope?' Polly prompted, uncomfortable with her sister's gratitude.

'Well, for a start, our sister doesn't go by that name. She is called Gemma Foster now. You'll be getting the agency report as well,' Ellie pointed out. 'Gemma was adopted but her parents, the Fosters, died and that landed her back into the foster system. She's twenty now and we just have to track her down.'

'Right.' Polly swallowed her disappointment that that was as far as the agency had got in their search for their sister and returned to an issue that was currently more on her mind. 'Remember you said that it usually takes at least six months to conceive—'

'That is *not* what I said!' Ellie sliced in, sounding infuriatingly like the newly qualified doctor she now was, having recently passed her finals. 'I said that was the average but obviously a woman *could* get pregnant the very first time she has sex without precautions. Nothing about conception is etched in stone. Why are you asking me about this again?'

'Just curious, that's all.'

'Don't be putting pressure on yourself in that department,' Ellie advised sagely. 'You're both young and healthy and you'll likely conceive sooner rather than later.'

The evening dress Polly was planning to wear was in autumnal shades of brown and gold with muted hints of tangerine. Her maid brought the amber set to her and she donned it with a frown because the necklace was every bit as weighty as she had feared and the exotic earrings were almost as bad. Fully dressed, her maid having bundled up her hair into an elaborate updo that gave her the height she lacked, she scrutinised her appearance, ready to admit that once again Hayat's advice had proved indispensable. The amber jewellery and the more mature hairstyle lent an impressive note of glamorous dignity to what might otherwise have been a rather plain outfit.

She did not see Rashad until she climbed into the limousine in which he awaited her and quite predictably, because he was never ever anything other than punctual to the minute, he was complaining that she had cut her timing too fine. As she turned towards him with a mischievous smile his attention settled on the collaret encircling her white throat and his lean, strong face snapped taut, sudden pallor accentuating his superb bone structure.

'You look stunning,' he murmured almost woodenly, turning his handsome face away, his jawline rigid.

'Is there something wrong?' Polly pressed uncertainly.

'No,' he asserted but not very convincingly.

The dinner was Polly's first public appearance at Rashad's side since the wedding and she was keen to get everything right. Hayat had prepared her well with a key sheet of useful information, listing names and faces and functions to ease her into the social evening.

Rashad, holding himself in rigid check, was temporarily drowning in his own memories. He could not see that amber necklace without also seeing Ferah wearing it. It had been her favourite, the colour of the semi-precious stones reflecting her brown eyes. During the drive to the embassy, he was steeped in the memories he had locked into a little box at the back of his head. He saw Ferah, laughing and smiling, full of energy and happiness at the outset of their marriage. Ferah before life had scarred her and fatally wounded her and *he* had let her down. Fierce discomfiture and guilt gripped him.

'Why did you choose that jewellery?' he asked with as much nonchalance as he could contrive.

'The amber gems match the dress perfectly,' Polly replied in some surprise.

'I prefer you in brighter colours,' Rashad imparted flatly, making a nonsense of the compliment he had initially paid her.

Polly squared her slim shoulders and gave a very slight shrug. 'I can't wear blue all the time. I have to ring the changes.'

Her soft mouth had settled into a surprisingly defiant line because she was annoyed with him. Didn't he realise how nervous she was at attending her first official function as the new Queen of Dharia? Didn't he appreciate that she needed support and encouragement rather than criticism? All right, he didn't like the dress, but he should have kept his opinion to himself, she reflected angrily.

Instead of clinging to his side as Rashad had expected, Polly vanished into the crush. It was obvious that she did not feel a need for his presence. Once or twice he heard her musical laughter and wondered what she was laughing at and, indeed, *who* she was laughing with. He told himself that he was grateful that she had found her own feet but, as a man whose first wife had never strayed more than a foot from him at such occasions and at all times followed his lead, he was perplexed and a shade threatened by Polly's independence.

'You've made a real find in the wife stakes with Polly,' a familiar voice drawled and Rashad's dark head spun.

'*Rio?*' he said in surprise. 'What are you doing back in Dharia?'

Rio Benedetti dealt him an amused smile. 'The Italian Ambassador knows we're friends and, as I had to check out a location for one of our hotels here, I volunteered to do my patriotic best to oil the wheels of diplomacy for him—'

'You mentioned Polly,' Rashad reminded him, unsettled to hear his wife's name on Rio's lips and at the same time to recognise Rio's admiration for her, because Rio was a notorious womaniser.

'Yes. She's lively and intelligent, a positive asset rather than the encumbrance you once feared a wife would be,' his old friend pointed out.

The faintest tinge of colour highlighted Rashad's hard cheekbones, for when he had been studying at Oxford with the younger man he had confided in him in a manner which, now that he was older and wiser, he would not risk repeating. 'I no longer fear that prospect,' he parried. 'In fact I am discovering that marriage suits me surprisingly well—'

Boldly impervious to hints, Rio laughed. 'Why are you surprised? She's gorgeous!'

'You seemed to be finding her sister equally attractive at our wedding,' Rashad commented, firmly moving the exchange away from his wife, whom he refused to discuss even with a close friend.

Rio grimaced. 'No, that went to hell in a handbasket for reasons I won't share. I'm afraid I landed the sister with the temperament of a shrew. By the looks of it, you got the sweet-natured one so be grateful for that reality,' he advised.

Rashad glanced across heads to where Polly stood engaged in animated dialogue with the British Ambassador. 'I'm very grateful,' he said grimly.

'Then why do you look anything but grateful?' Rio asked very drily.

Rashad truly didn't know how to answer that direct question. He shrugged a broad shoulder in smouldering silence. His brilliant dark eyes were hooded, his teeming thoughts full of conflict. He was well aware that he was being unreasonable. He had wanted a confident, independent woman as a wife and he had got one. Why was he now wishing that she would cling just a little? Seek him out for advice and guidance? Flash her eyes restively round the room, looking anxiously for him as if she needed and missed him? Why was he being so perverse? So illogical?

He invited Rio to dine with him at the palace and without hesitation chose the same evening that Polly invariably spent with her grandparents, Hakim and his wife. The less Polly was exposed to Rio, the better, he decided with pious resolve.

\* \* \*

'You did incredibly well tonight,' Rashad told Polly on the drive back to the palace. 'You didn't once look to me for backup either.'

A sensation of unease niggled at the base of Polly's skull. Why did he make that sound more like a negative than a plus? Why had he kept his distance throughout the evening? Was she ever going to understand the man she had married? The minute she believed she had solved the mystery of Rashad he would do something she wasn't expecting and confuse her again.

'I thought you wanted me to be independent—'

'I do,' Rashad confirmed. 'I can't always be by your side and sometimes you will have to attend such events alone.'

'So why am I *still* getting a mixed message here?' Polly queried a shade tartly.

Rashad shrugged a broad shoulder as he sprang out of the limo, relieved to be back on palace ground. He knew he was being difficult, he knew he was being too emotional but he was a seething tangle of conflicting feelings inside himself and struggling to hide the fact. In truth, Polly had shone like the brightest of stars at the dinner and without the smallest help from him. He had been very impressed by the natural warmth she exuded. Yet she had still somehow managed to maintain a certain amount of royal distance and formality, a formality which in no way came naturally to her for she was one of the most unstudied personalities he had ever met. In short she had contrived to be the public success that Ferah had always longed to be but had never managed to be. That cruel comparison stopped Rashad in his tracks and yet another surge of guilt and regret bit into him.

Polly sped after Rashad into the palace, wondering what the heck was wrong with him. By the time she actually caught up with him he was poised by the window in their bedroom. He flashed night-dark brooding eyes over her lovely face as she entered. Brilliant dark golden eyes screened by ridiculously long black lashes. Her heart skipped a sudden beat, her breath catching in her throat. Her hand flew up to her constricted throat and rested on the weight of the amber necklace. With a sigh she stretched her fingers round to the clasp at her nape to undo it.

'Let me,' Rashad urged, taking her by surprise as he strode forward.

The ornate collaret lifted and he settled it down in a careless heap on a tall dresser. 'Don't wear it again,' he urged her in a roughened voice.

'Wear what?' Polly queried as she reached up and unhooked each earring in swift succession before looking at him in the mirror for further clarification.

'The ambers. I'll buy you another set,' he promised curtly, his lean dark face shuttered.

Her violet eyes kindled with curiosity. 'What's wrong with this set?' she asked bluntly.

Rashad tensed, dark lashes sweeping down to screen his expression. 'It was Ferah's favourite.'

'Oh...' Polly gasped as if he had punched her and deprived her lungs of breath, and in a way that was exactly what he had done. He didn't like seeing her wearing his first wife's much-loved jewellery? What was she supposed to take from that admission?

'It awakens unfortunate memories,' Rashad declared abruptly.

He had loved his first wife and clearly he couldn't bear any reminder of her, Polly assumed, thoroughly discomfited by that awareness. 'I'm your wife now,' she reminded him flatly, wishing that that timely reminder didn't sound quite so childish.

'I'm well aware of that,' Rashad said drily.

'And maybe I don't brush up as nicely as Ferah did in the ambers but you've just made me want to wear them every darned day!' Polly admitted in a helplessly aggressive tone. 'After all, she is gone and I'm here and I have feelings too!'

'This is a crazy conversation.' A questioning black brow elevated, doubtless urging her to think more carefully about what she was saying.

But Polly had had enough and she didn't feel like pretending or indeed lying to save face. 'No, I'm a possessive woman. Either you're mine or you're *still* hers!' Polly fired at him in angry challenge.

'Ferah is my past as you are my present and my future,' Rashad countered in exasperation.

Polly's violet eyes widened and glittered and she planted her hand truculently on one slender jutting hip. 'But your past is raining on my present so I'm not getting a fair deal,' she told him accusingly.

Rashad groaned out loud, frustration gripping him. 'What am I supposed to do about that? I cannot help my past. I cannot forget my memories—'

'No…' Polly conceded. 'But you could share them.'

'*Share* them?' Rashad exclaimed, an expression of appalled fascination stamping his lean, darkly handsome face. 'What man would do that?'

'A man who wants a normal relationship with his wife. If your memories are coming between us, you need to share them,' Polly told him abruptly, for in actuality she was none too sure of the worth of what she was proposing. After all, she didn't really *want* to think about Ferah. She preferred to forget that his first wife had ever existed, which was probably distinctly mean and ungenerous of her. Would it be worse for her to have Ferah fleshed out as a person? Ferah, the woman he had loved who must have loved him too?

'My memories are *not* coming between us,' Rashad assured her with brooding ferocity. 'And I prefer to keep my memories to myself—'

'Oh, tell me something I don't already know,' Polly scoffed in a helpless rush of bitterness. 'It's like when you were made someone locked you up internally and threw away the key!'

'I am what I am—'

'Too set in your ways to change?' Polly skimmed back thinly.

'We have only been married for a couple of months. What sort of miraculous transformation were you expecting this soon?' Rashad derided.

Polly paled at that sardonic recap and intonation and turned away. 'I'm going to bed.'

'I'm going for a ride,' Rashad told her between gritted teeth.

'No, you're walking out on me again because I've said things you don't want to deal with!' Polly condemned angrily.

Rashad settled stormy dark golden eyes on her and froze. 'Very well. I will stay.'

To talk? To share? Or to prove her wrong in her contention that he'd walk away sooner than deal with difficult issues? With a determined little wriggle, Polly unzipped her dress while watching Rashad shed his clothing. Watching him made her mouth run dry, all that sleek bronzed flesh overlying lean, hard muscle being exposed. Flushing at her thoughts, she pulled on a robe and went into the bathroom to remove her makeup.

Now he was furious with her, she ruminated wryly. Golden fury had blazed like the heat of the sun in his beautiful eyes. But he wouldn't admit that he was angry. Nor would he raise his voice or lose his temper. His absolute control of his emotions mocked her trembling hands because she was so wound up she felt as though she might explode with the powerful anxious feelings racing round inside her.

Seeing her in his first wife's jewellery roused 'unfortunate memories'. It made him angry too. Had he watched her tonight in that wretched amber necklace and wished she were Ferah? What else was she supposed to think?

Rashad studied Polly's slender figure. The silk of the robe outlined the rounded curve of her derriere and delicately shaped her pouting breasts, hinting at her prominent nipples. His reaction was instantaneous and it infuriated him but there it was: the lust to take, the lust to possess gripped him almost every time he looked at his wife. The strength of that craving disturbed him as much as his loss of self-discipline. Hard as a rock, he stepped into the shower and put the jets on cold but it didn't help because all that out-of-control emotion washing about inside him like a dangerous rip tide threatening to drag him down only heightened his arousal, exacerbating his need to be close to Polly in the only way he knew.

Share his memories? Was Polly crazy to suggest such a thing? He did not want to relive his unhappy marriage to Ferah. The two women could not have been more different, he conceded heavily. Polly wanted to talk about sensitive issues but Ferah had refused to talk and had brooded on her disappointments until she was overflowing with the bitterness and self-pity that had eventually plunged her into long depressive episodes. How could he even consider sharing that unlovely truth with Polly?

Polly undid the robe and wondered if it would be a little ridiculous for her to put on a nightdress because they had had a disagreement. When she normally wore nothing to bed but her own skin a nightdress would be like making a statement, wouldn't it be? Ultra-sensitive and on edge, she glanced uncertainly at Rashad as he strode out of the bathroom. The air positively crackled when she collided with burning dark golden eyes and she noticed, really couldn't help noticing, his condition.

'Yes, I want you,' Rashad intoned thickly. 'But then…I *always* want you.'

'Don't say it like you wish you didn't!' Polly exclaimed, her mouth running dry, her heartbeat speeding up.

'It can be inconvenient—'

'What's a little inconvenience?' she whispered, achingly aware of him, struggling to remind herself that he hadn't dealt with her demand for more information and that she should be light on understanding while playing it cool and offended.

'I couldn't be gentle in the mood I'm in—'

Polly tried and failed to swallow. There was a wildness in his eyes, a gritty roughened edge to his dark deep drawl and, in the strangest way imaginable, she welcomed that hint that he was not as much in control as he usually was. It was almost as though a barrier had come down inside him, one of several barriers that kept her at a determined distance. 'I might not necessarily *need* gentle right now...'

Without the smallest hesitation, Rashad crossed the space between them in one stride, both arms snaking round her to bring her crashing up against his hot, muscular body. His sensual mouth feasted on hers with a ferocity that suggested she could be the only thing standing between him and insanity and she gloried in a fervour that empowered her at a moment when her self-esteem had taken a battering. After all, it was hard to be proud of being Rashad's consolation prize in the bride stakes, the replacement wife virtually forced on him by the Dharian people.

'I *burn* to be with you,' Rashad growled, erotic energy radiating from him as he brought her down on the bed, his hunger unleashed and sizzling with unashamed intensity. 'Every minute of the day. My appetite for you consumes me.'

She would have told him that that cut both ways but his mouth crushed hers again and the taste of him was like an aphrodisiac, the plunge of his tongue making her body arch up in a wave of shivering delight that shot a fire storm of response through her veins. There was a ripping sound as he extracted her impatiently from the entangling folds of the silk robe. Long, knowing fingers zeroed straight in on the slick pink flesh at the heart of her and she jerked and moaned out loud, on the edge of spontaneously combusting with excitement.

Rashad flipped her over and drew her up on her knees. With a heartfelt growl of satisfaction he sank into her in a single compelling thrust. She was stretched almost to the point of pain but simultaneously the raw pleasure stormed through her nerve endings like a healing drug. He took her hard and fast and that sense of being on an edge flung her up onto an endless high of breathless excitement. Carnal pleasure gripped her bone and sinew. His lack of control thrilled her because she knew that she wasn't in control either. In any case, this was Rashad and she loved him, trusted him, *needed* him, and that his savage hunger for her should be even stronger when he was angry and troubled comforted her. After all that same primal need to connect with him at such times was just as powerful and driving for her.

She was riding a ravishing surge of excitement when a skilled hand rubbed against her throbbing bud of pleasure and the world burst into Technicolor fireworks behind her eyelids. She jerked and cried out, caught up in a rolling climax that detonated deep in her pelvis and totally wiped her out. When she collapsed back down on the bed, Rashad rolled her into his arms and lay there with her, struggling for breath, his heart still thundering against her.

'I'm sorry,' Rashad gritted unevenly. 'I was rough, selfish. I am truly sorry—'

'No...I liked it...'

Long fingers pushed up her chin to force her eyes to meet his, his concern evaporating to be replaced by the beginnings of sheer masculine awe. 'You *liked* it?' he whispered wonderingly.

'Uh-huh,' Polly confirmed, her colour rising inexorably beneath that stunned appraisal.

'Sometimes I feel as though there's a crazy storm rising inside me—'

'Tension, emotion...'

'That I've failed to get under control,' Rashad pronounced, his beautiful mouth tightening with dissatisfaction.

'But you don't need to control it, not with me. With me, you don't have to put up a front, you don't have to impress.' Polly wrapped a possessive arm round his lean, damp body, small fingers smoothing down soothingly over his ribcage. 'I want you to be yourself.'

'Be careful what you wish for.' Rashad turned his tousled dark head away from her. 'Ferah chose to die sooner than remain with me,' he said flatly, no emotion whatsoever in the statement.

Completely taken aback by that shockingly sudden change of topic, Polly tensed. *'Chose?'* she queried with a frown.

'A few weeks before she was bitten by the snake she took an overdose. Fortunately she was found in time and I arranged for her to have treatment and therapy but sadly it wasn't enough. When she was bitten she concealed the bite until it was too late for the antidote to work,' Rashad revealed. 'She died in my arms. She told me that she was setting me free...'

Polly was appalled, belatedly grasping why any memory of Ferah was liable to upset him. She almost spoke her mind to say that she thought that that was a dreadfully cruel and martyred thing to have said to him in such circumstances but common sense made her bite her lip rather than speak in insensitive haste. 'Setting you free?' she whispered instead.

'Free to marry another woman, one who could give me a child as she could not,' Rashad extended curtly. 'She knew her father had been trying to persuade me to divorce her and take another wife and that I had refused—'

'Her own *father* was willing to do that to her?' Polly pressed in disgust.

'All my uncle saw was the end game and that was the restoration of the monarchy. He saw a king with an heir in tow as a safer bet than one with a barren wife,' Rashad advanced bitterly. 'Ferah knew how he felt because he told her that it was her duty to let me go. She was already depressed. All she ever wanted was to be a mother and when that was denied her she felt worthless. Being made to feel like a burden as well was too much for her. She wasn't a strong person.'

'I'm so sorry,' Polly muttered, feeling inadequate because he had told her a much more unhappy story than she had expected and for the first time she understood that Rashad had been as much wounded by his first marriage as he had been by the traumatic changes and injuries inflicted on him by his dysfunctional childhood. The sheer extent of the losses he had endured turned her stomach over sickly, making her feel outrageously naïve.

'I should've given her more support. It's my fault that she died,' Rashad murmured with grave simplicity.

'It *wasn't* your fault!' Polly argued vehemently. 'She was depressed. You got her professional help. What more could you have done? By the sound of it, her own family did nothing to help her recover!'

Rashad stretched out with a heavy sigh. 'It's in the past and can't be changed, *aziz*. Let us leave it there.'

But although Polly sealed her lips on further comment she couldn't leave it there because she felt ashamed that she had come over all jealous and possessive about his attachment to Ferah and his memories of his first marriage. Her sister had tried to warn her that Rashad had been through the emotional grinder in the past and she hadn't really listened. He had also trained himself to control his emotions and keep his secrets and in his position that was hardly surprising. That he had let the barriers down just for a few minutes with her was a promising sign, she told herself with determined positivity.

# CHAPTER NINE

POLLY SHIFTED IN the early hours, partially wakening to the sound of Rashad having a terse conversation with someone on the phone. Blinking, she turned over, eyes drowsy in the half-light before dawn as he put the phone down again and sat up.

'There was an incident on the border during the night.' He sighed, raking long brown fingers through his sleep-tousled jet-black hair. 'A man was shot but mercifully *not* killed. I'll be in meetings all day trying to calm this down, but first I have to fly out there and get the facts.'

He dropped a kiss on her brow and urged her to go back to sleep. A few hours later, Polly rolled out of bed with her usual energy and then stopped dead as a roiling wave of sick dizziness assailed her. There was nothing she could do but rush for the bathroom where she knelt on the cold tiled floor to be ignominiously sick. In the aftermath, she felt weak and shaky and it was a few minutes before she took the risk of standing up again.

She couldn't have fallen pregnant so quickly, she reasoned with herself as she stepped into the shower, needing to feel clean from head to toe. Ellie had said the average conception took around six months but that it could just as easily take longer. No, it was much more likely that she had caught some bug or eaten something at dinner that had disagreed with her digestion. Even so, she thought that it would be sensible to consult the palace doctor.

She dried her hair and got dressed, wondering if Rashad would be gone as long as he had feared. No matter what was on his agenda he generally managed to share breakfast with her and she had learned to cherish their quiet moments together. Her period was a week overdue, she recalled with sudden reluctance, but she hadn't paid any heed to that because she'd suspected that the radical change of diet and climate was playing havoc with her system. After all, last month she had been early so possibly this month her cycle would be late to compensate for that.

Hayat awaited her in the reception room next door with a list of Polly's phone calls and her emails, each starred in terms of what Hayat deemed important. That her sister, Ellie's call only rated the bottom of the list was telling. She learned that she had received an invitation to open the new wing of the hospital in Kashan and asked Hayat if she would arrange an appointment for her with Dr Wasem.

'You are unwell?' Hayat questioned, studying her with a frown.

'No. I simply wish to consult the doctor,' Polly replied.

After a busy half-hour of tests and an examination

with Dr Wasem Polly discovered that she *was* pregnant. Her idle musings to that effect were proven when she had least expected it. In truth she was stunned because Rashad's admission about Ferah's sterility and his laid-back assumption allied to her own that it would take months for her to conceive had all combined to make her look on motherhood as a distinctly distant possibility. Instead it had suddenly become her new reality.

'I am honoured beyond words to break this news to you,' Dr Wasem informed her, his huge smile warm with genuine pleasure on her behalf.

'I'll tell Rashad tonight so I would be grateful if this remains confidential,' Polly responded tactfully, well aware that in the claustrophobic gossip mill of the royal household the good doctor probably wanted to shout her announcement from the rooftops.

'Of course.'

Polly positively floated out of his ultra-modern surgery on the ground floor of the palace. A baby, Rashad's baby. He would be so happy, so *relieved*, she reflected ruefully. He had lived through the pressure of a childless first marriage and all the fertility testing that had gone with it, and she knew that he considered the entire process stressful and potentially disastrous. Now he would be able to relax and forget about worrying, she thought tenderly.

A radiant smile lit Polly's face as she began to formulate plans for the rest of the day. She phoned her sister first and beamed at Ellie's shout of delighted anticipation. Afterwards she called her grandfather's home to speak to her grandmother and ask if she could visit them on another evening. She held back her pregnancy news, wanting to share that with Rashad first.

'That would be best,' Dursa told her granddaughter in her halting English. 'Hakim is travelling with the King and will be away until late and your grandfather would not like to miss your visit.'

Her single social engagement cancelled, Polly decided to spend the rest of the day painting. She had her regular language lesson first, of course, and then spent another hour studying Dharian history and culture. The more she learned about every aspect of Dharian life, the easier she found it to understand Rashad's concerns and share them. It was particularly interesting to learn about the heroine of the legend, the saintly Queen Zariyah. Why *had* her mother named her Zariyah at birth? Her grandfather, Hakim, thought it might have been because the name was revered in Dharia and her mother had wanted to give her that link to her father's heritage, but Polly thought it was just as likely that her mother had simply thought the name was pretty. Evidently she had not appreciated or had possibly not cared that the name was almost never used out of respect for the original Zariyah. Now the world had turned full circle, Polly acknowledged, for while it was known that she was called Polly the media routinely referred to her as Queen Zariyah.

'You're going to paint,' Hayat said unnecessarily when Polly appeared in the loose sundress she usually wore for her sessions.

Polly nodded, wondering why Hayat was staring at

her, her dark eyes cool, her face stiff. Had she offended the other woman in some way? Polly pushed the concern to the back of her mind because she was not in the mood to tackle what would be a difficult conversation. In fact she kept on wanting to smile in the most stupid inane way because she was so happy about the baby she carried. As she relaxed into that startling concept she was finally allowing herself to think about what it would mean to have a child and become a parent.

Certainly, she hoped that she would manage to be a better parent than her own mother had contrived to be. Although she felt guilty feeling judgemental like that, she had had a great deal more compassion for her late mother since she had learned the tragic circumstances of her own birth. Yet Annabel Dixon had moved on from the loss of her husband by very quickly conceiving another child and once again landing the responsibility for that child onto her own mother's shoulders. Polly sighed with regret. It seemed that her mother had led a tumultuous, lonely and unhappy life, for she had never managed to sustain a lasting relationship with any one of her daughters' fathers. She wanted something very different for her own life and her own child, she conceded ruefully. She wanted love and stability and two parents for her baby, so that her child could feel safe and supported as he or she grew up.

The air-conditioned cool of the room set aside for her to use as a studio was welcome. There were two unfinished canvases on easels, one a painstaking watercolour in Polly's signature dreamy pastels of the star-shaped pool on the ground floor, the second a sunset in oils of the desert landscape. The second painting was a new departure for Polly. The colours were more adventurous, the brush strokes bolder, possibly expressing the many changes that had engulfed her since she first came to Dharia, she acknowledged thoughtfully.

And yet had she had a choice there was nothing she would change, she reflected while she painted. Rashad had transformed her life. Her gaze flickered to the ring on her wedding finger, the miniaturised fire-opal ring, and she smiled giddily, marvelling that her mother's legacy, inapt as it might have been, had nonetheless reunited her with her grandparents and allowed her to meet Rashad. Gorgeous but often unfathomable Rashad. He was passionate, clever and driven, sexy beyond words, everything she had not even known she wanted in a man until she met him. But he was also a multifaceted challenge with hidden and dangerous depths and that worried her, for she herself was not introspective and pretty much wore her feelings on the surface.

As the heat of day began to fade Polly went off to shower and change into the blue dress Rashad particularly admired. If he made it back in time she would tell him about the baby over dinner, otherwise over a late supper. In fact it didn't matter how late he got back, she would wait up.

When she reappeared, Hayat was waiting for her again. 'I'm afraid there has been an oversight. The King's friend, Mr Benedetti, is about to arrive to join him for dinner and the King is not here—'

Polly frowned, knowing how important the art of

hospitality was to Rashad and how very rude a last-minute cancellation would be. 'I'll dine with him and explain.'

Hayat gave her a bright admiring smile. 'You are daring—'

Polly raised a brow. 'How?'

'To dine alone with a man who is not your husband.'

Polly laughed. 'Neither my husband nor I are that old-fashioned,' she asserted with confidence.

Rio Benedetti was charm personified, soothing her concern that he might be offended by Rashad's absence with an easy flow of entertaining conversation stamped with an occasional subtle query about Ellie, which made Polly's sisterly antenna prickle with curiosity. After all, Ellie had evinced no similar desire to discuss Rio with Polly, claiming that she had only appeared to enjoy Rio's company at the wedding out of politeness and hadn't actually liked him at all. In fact she had dismissed him as a player with sleazy chat-up lines. Somehow, Rio had got entirely on the wrong side of her spirited sister.

The Italian billionaire did not keep her late and Polly was curled up in a corner couch on her own with a book by the time Rashad strode through the door after eleven that evening. The instant that she saw his stormy dark face, she knew that he was in a temper and concern indented her brow.

'What's happened?' she exclaimed, coming upright in her bare feet, noting that lines of strain bracketed his mouth.

Rashad regarded her in astonishment. She had spent

an entire evening alone with an infamous womaniser, utterly disregarding Hayat's advice. The minute Rashad had received that news he had assumed that his wife found Rio so compellingly attractive that she had decided to throw away the rule book and that thought, that *fear* had simply spawned an ungovernable rage that far outran any emotion Rashad had ever felt. Exhausted as he already was by an endless day of repetitive diplomacy and incessant meetings, Hayat's phone call had incensed him.

'Why didn't you listen to Hayat when she advised you not to dine alone with Rio?'

Polly tilted her chin. 'She didn't advise me *not* to do it, she just said it was daring. I thought that was nonsense when I was only trying to be polite and considerate. Telling him you were unavailable when he was literally on the way here would have been very rude and as he is a close friend of yours I thought you wouldn't want that—'

'Or perhaps the temptation of having Rio all to yourself was too great!' Rashad flung at her rawly. 'He is notoriously sought after by women.'

'Not by my sister,' Polly remarked abstractedly, suddenly recognising that Rashad, whether he knew it or not, was consumed by jealousy. 'You really don't have to be jealous—'

*'Jealous?'* The word hit Rashad like a brick thrown on glass, shattering what little control he retained. 'I have never been jealous over a woman in my life!'

'Sleep on it and then think about it,' Polly advised, losing patience and angry with him because she had been eager to tell him about their baby and now he had wrecked the mood with his temper. He was so volatile, so possessive. On what planet did he live that he believed she could be so eager to make love with him while planning to betray him with his closest friend? Had she been too eager? Was that the problem? Did he think she was some sort of natural-born wanton who could not be trusted in the radius of any attractive man? A dark flush of fuming humiliation reddened Polly's face and chest and she turned her head away from him to walk past him.

Long, lean fingers closed round her wrist to intercept her. 'Where are you going?'

'I've got nothing more to say to you.' Polly yanked her arm free and, feeling the prickle of angry, hurt tears stinging her eyes, she fled past him into the corridor. How could Rashad talk to her like that? How could he even see her in such a light? Was this her reward for matching that dark, passionate intensity of his?

'Polly...'

'I *hate* you!' Polly flung over her shoulder as she started down the stairs that led to their bedroom.

And it was that twisting round to make that final response that unbalanced her. She missed a step and lurched. Her feverish grab at the stone bannister failed and she fell, instinctively turning her body into herself as she had been taught to fall from a horse. Her hip hit stone and she cried out in pain and then the back of her head struck a step and she knew no more...

# CHAPTER TEN

A FAINT MOAN parted Polly's lips because her head was aching and she came awake with a sense of frightened confusion. Her eyes opened on an unfamiliar room. She saw a bewildering number of faces, blinked and registered that she was in a hospital bed with the side bars raised.

'Polly?' Rashad breathed tautly, springing out of the chair beside her.

'What?' she mumbled because moving her lips felt like too much effort. 'My head's sore…my hip.'

As she focused blearily on him he stepped back to allow the medical staff to attend to her and she wondered why he looked so tired and why the sun was shining into the room when only minutes ago it had been dark. A nurse checked her blood pressure and gave her a drink while a doctor asked her a series of questions. Her attention, however, stayed squarely on Rashad while she struggled to recall what had happened to her. Black stubble accentuated his stubborn passionate mouth, his luxuriant hair was dishevelled, his eyes shadowed, his powerful anxiety unconcealed.

Recalling her fall on the stairs and the argument that had preceded it taxed her concentration and then, with a sudden whoosh of awareness, all that fell away on the shocking surge of apprehension that shot through her. She pressed a stricken hand against her stomach.

'My baby?' she gasped fearfully.

Rashad strode forward and rested a hand over hers in a soothing gesture. 'Our baby is fine—'

'For the moment. There has been no bleeding but you must rest. The next twenty-four hours are crucial to your recovery,' the grey-haired doctor told her firmly as he urged her to lie still.

Rashad's hand was trembling over hers and just as she noticed that he withdrew it in a sudden gesture and dug it into the pocket of his trousers. He *knew* that she was pregnant; he knew about the baby. She assumed that Dr Wasem had told him after she fell and knocked herself out. Polly closed her eyes, guessing just how guilty Rashad would be feeling. She was still furious with him but she knew his habit of blaming himself for everything bad that happened around him. If she lost their baby he would never forgive himself for upsetting her. How could she be furious with him and yet aching inside herself for what he was feeling at the same time? It was that crazy conundrum called love, she decided ruefully.

While the doctor talked to her about the concussion she had sustained, Polly tried to think clearly and focus but it was no use, she simply *couldn't*. Both her head and her body ached. The mental confusion and the extreme fatigue the doctor had warned her about were steadily closing in on her because there was far too much to think about and it was infinitely easier to close it all out just then and drift. She still had her baby, she reflected with passionate relief, and that was the last clear thought she had.

Rashad paced the silent room. He had tidied himself up in response to Hakim's pleas but he had not eaten, he had not slept. How could he? His temper, that wild surging rage he couldn't always control, could have killed Polly. He looked at her, lying so still in the bed, white-blonde hair tumbling across the pillow, her face showing a little colour now, no longer that wan grey that had terrified him. She was so fragile, so precious...

And the baby? Rashad was still stunned by that development, that incredulous realisation that, if there was nothing medically amiss to prevent it, a pregnancy could happen so quickly, so easily, so...so *normally*, he recognised. He hadn't expected that, hadn't prepared for it either. In fact he had pessimistically assumed that although they might conceive a child eventually it would undoubtedly take a long time. Once again he had made the mistake of allowing past disappointment and disillusionment to influence his expectations in the present. And how could she ever forgive him for that?

He was fatally flawed, almost programmed to disappoint Polly. He had even failed to protect her from Hayat's malice. *'Either you're mine or you're still hers,'* Polly had flung at him, referring to Ferah, and he could see that now—could see that he had failed to make peace with the past and move on to embrace a wife far superior in every way to his first. And if it was wrong and disrespectful to think that then it was better to be wrong but at least rational enough to recognise that truth. Fate had rained gold on him when he least deserved it and he had virtually thrown away the opportunity he had been given, he conceded grimly.

'You *must* eat and rest, Your Majesty,' Hakim whispered fiercely from the doorway. 'How can you support your wife if you are exhausted?'

'As always, the voice of reason,' Rashad conceded wearily, but his every instinct still warred against leaving Polly alone. At least while he watched over her he could actually feel as though he was *doing* something to help, but in reality, while she was under medical supervision, he could only be an onlooker.

Polly wakened and slowly savoured the strength returning to her body. She pushed down the bedding and tugged up her gown to squint at the horrid blue-black bruising covering her hip and stretching down her thigh. Better her hip than her stomach, she decided as a nurse came in and gently scolded her for sitting up in bed without help. Suddenly she was surrounded by staff again and she was changed and the bed was changed and then breakfast was ushered in.

An hour later, Rashad arrived, sleek and shaven in a beautifully cut dark suit. He looked fantastically handsome and considerably more groomed and calm than he had the day before. His stunning dark golden eyes immediately sought hers and instinctively she evaded his gaze, too full of conflict to meet it. He had revealed his lack of trust in her. He had believed that even though they were married she could still be tempted by another man and that she could be unfaithful. How could she overlook or forgive that?

'I have a lot to say to you,' Rashad murmured tautly. 'But first your grandparents are waiting to see you and you should see them now to reassure them.'

'Of course,' she muttered uncertainly, wondering what he had to say to her, wondering what she would say to him.

'If your medical team agree, I can take you home later.'

Polly compressed her lips in silence.

'Hayat has now gone home to her mother. She won't be returning to the palace staff,' he told her in a harsh clipped undertone. 'I was foolish to trust her near you—'

Polly studied him directly for the first time. 'What on earth are you talking about?'

His lean, strong face went rigid. 'Apparently Hayat was angry and jealous that I had married you and she decided to cause trouble between us…and in that she succeeded,' he divulged grudgingly. 'I told her to cancel that dinner with Rio before I left the palace the day before yesterday. But she didn't cancel it. She set you up instead, set us *both* up…challenging you to dine alone with him, knowing that I am *not*—at heart— the liberated male I must strive to be for your sake…'

Polly was shaken by that explanation. 'But why would Hayat be angry and jealous? Were you involved with her before I came into your life?'

Rashad frowned. 'Of course not…she is Ferah's kid sister. I found it hard to warm to her personality, though—'

'Hayat's your sister-in-law?' Polly exclaimed in disbelief. 'Why did nobody tell *me* that?'

'It wasn't a secret. I didn't think it was important. I didn't want to discriminate against her either because she is, or *was*, very efficient.' Rashad lifted his handsome dark head high and expelled his breath in an audible rush, frustration and regret tensing his lean dark face. 'I made a mistake in allowing her access to you and I'm afraid you paid for my lack of judgement.'

Long lashes fluttering down, Polly cloaked her eyes to conceal her incredulity. How could he not have warned her about his familial relationship with the other woman? She remembered Hayat admitting that she had watched her sister break her heart over her inability to conceive and, remembering her own unease around the attractive brunette, she swallowed back angry words of condemnation. His first wife's little sister, someone who would be challenged to wish Rashad's second wife a long and happy life after Ferah's tragic fate.

'Hayat admitted that she resented my remarriage and our happiness,' Rashad volunteered tautly. 'I should have foreseen that likelihood and her spite.'

'Well, it's done and dusted now,' Polly pointed out curtly, because she was annoyed at what she had learnt. 'She's left the staff and as it happens I'm all right—'

'*Inshallah,*' Rashad breathed, rising to leave as her grandparents bustled in, all smiles and concern, to present her with a very large basket of fruit. Their caring and affectionate presence was exactly what she needed to soothe her ruffled feelings at that moment. She received a hail of anxious words and a hug from her grandmother and a quiet squeeze on the shoulder from Hakim, who wasn't given to drama.

Rashad came to collect her from the hospital. He explained that there were crowds waiting for a glimpse of her outside the hospital and they left by a rear entrance.

'Why won't you look at me?' Rashad pressed on the drive back to the palace.

'I'm angry with you,' Polly admitted curtly.

Rashad released his breath on a slow hiss. 'Of course you are. I spoiled what should have been a special moment—'

She assumed he meant that she had missed the chance to tell him privately about their baby.

'Not only that,' she broke in jaggedly. 'You behaved as if I was some kind of harlot who couldn't be trusted alone in a room with a man!'

'I deeply regret the way in which I behaved,' Rashad admitted levelly. 'If I could go back and eradicate what I said I would…but I cannot.'

Colour scoring her cheekbones, Polly chewed the soft underside of her lower lip and made no response. What could she say? She *knew* he regretted it.

'I didn't like being confronted with the reality that you could think of me like that.'

'We will talk when we get home. I don't want to be interrupted,' Rashad murmured tautly.

A tense silence fell and Polly did nothing to break

it. In truth she was as annoyed with herself as she was with him. Wasn't she usually a forgiving person? But what Rashad had said had struck at the very heart of their relationship and had deeply wounded her because she loved him. He didn't know that she loved him. He hadn't asked her to love him. And she wouldn't tell him because he would assume that she craved some kind of matching response from him when she did not. She didn't want Rashad to feel that he had to pretend to feel more for her than he actually did. It would make him uncomfortable and he would be hopeless at faking it. Over the long term, honesty and common sense would be safer than emotional outpourings that would only muddy the water between them.

Tearful staff greeted her on their knees in the entrance hall. She was deeply touched by that demonstration of affection. Rashad's people were very emotional and unafraid to show it. She marvelled that they had a king who worked so hard at concealing every emotion he experienced as if emotion were something to be ashamed of.

'The doctors advised that you rest now,' Rashad reminded her as they entered the private wing of the palace.

Flowers were everywhere in the airy drawing room and piles of gifts cluttered every surface. 'What on earth…?' Polly began to ask.

'As soon as it was known that you had suffered an accident the flowers and the presents came flooding in,' Rashad explained. 'There has been no official announcement of your pregnancy, nor will there be for some time, but I suspect rumours are already on the streets. There were too many servants and guards hovering after your accident and Dr Wasem's anxiety on your behalf was unmistakeable.'

'And what about you?' Polly whispered. 'How did you react?'

'It was the worst moment of my life,' Rashad declared without hesitation, his strong jaw clenching hard. 'Until I realised you were still breathing I was afraid you were dead—'

'Or that I would lose the baby,' she slotted in wryly.

'I could have borne that better than the loss of you,' Rashad parried harshly. 'There could always be another baby…but there is only one *you*. And you are irreplaceable.'

There was a little red devil in Polly's brain because somehow she was not in the mood to listen while he made such comforting complimentary statements. 'No, I'm not,' she disagreed, turning her violet eyes onto his lean, perfect profile. 'You would still have women queuing up to marry you and become your Queen and the mother of your children.'

'Two dead predecessors in the role would limit my appeal somewhat. I would seem like a regular Bluebeard.'

A startled laugh was wrenched from Polly. 'There is that,' she conceded, turning away to hesitantly finger a tiny velvet soft frog toy that had been unwrapped.

It was undeniably a toy intended for their unborn child. Her eyes prickled with tears. Her most private secret had become public and she had been deprived of the right to share the news of her first pregnancy with her husband. She dashed the tears away with an angry hand, scolding herself for getting upset by gifts intended to express heartfelt good wishes.

'I wanted to tell you myself,' she framed gruffly.

'I know…I screwed it up,' Rashad bit out jerkily.

'Maybe we both did,' Polly muttered heavily. 'In a marriage it takes two to screw up. Whatever way you look at it, it's a partnership.'

'No,' Rashad disagreed. 'I didn't allow us to be a partnership. I have no experience of a marriage of equals. I have no experience of sharing feelings or memories. I have always had to keep such things to myself but with you…' He hesitated, shooting a look at her from shimmering dark golden eyes. 'With you, my control breaks down and things escape.'

Polly studied him and her heart felt as though he were crushing it because she bled for him at that moment, seeing him boy and man, rigorously disciplined to hold every feeling in, never allowed to be natural. 'That's not necessarily a bad thing,' she whispered shakily.

'It *was* a bad thing when I confronted you about your dinner with Rio,' Rashad pointed out heavily. 'I was…irrational. Rage engulfed me. I could not bear to think of you enjoying his company or admiring him. You do not need to tell me that I'm too possessive of you…I *know* it. I have never known such jealousy before and it ate me alive—'

'Well,' Polly murmured, inching a little closer because his sheer emotional intensity drew her like a flame on an icy day, 'I understand a little better now. But it upset me a lot that you seemed to distrust me—'

Rashad swung back to her, his stunning eyes bright with regret. 'But that is what is so illogical about it. I *do* trust you and Rio is my best friend and I know he would not betray me but *still* those feelings overwhelmed me!'

Polly brushed his arm with hesitant fingers. 'Because you're not used to dealing with that kind of stuff. You're on a learning curve.'

'I *hurt* you. If it hurts you I do not want to be on that curve,' he breathed rawly.

'But not expressing what you feel makes you a powder keg, which is more dangerous,' Polly argued.

'It won't ever happen again,' Rashad intoned. 'I will be on my guard now.'

'But that's not what I want,' Polly admitted ruefully.

'I have kept too many secrets from you,' Rashad confessed, striding over to the window, deeply troubled by his sense of disloyalty to his first wife's memory but accepting that such honesty was necessary. 'My first marriage was very unhappy—'

'But you said you loved her,' Polly reminded him in complete surprise.

'At the outset when we were teenagers trying to behave like grown-ups, we clung to each other for that was all we had. She was my first love even though we had very little in common. I made the best of it that I could but I did not love Ferah as she loved me,' Rashad declared with strong regret etched in his lean, darkly handsome features. 'And she *knew* it. Her inability to conceive was a constant source of stress for both of us and she became a deeply troubled woman. Nothing I said or did comforted her. I tried many times to get through to her and I failed. What love there was died until by the end we were like two strangers forced to live together.'

Polly stared at him in shock, utterly unprepared for that revelation.

'Now you know the *real* truth,' Rashad completed grimly.

'But…' she began uncertainly, frowning in bewilderment.

'For the last five years of our marriage I was celibate. That side of our marriage ended the day Ferah learned that she could not have a child. She turned away from me,' he revealed curtly, his difficulty in making that admission etched in the strained lines of his lean dark features. 'I felt unwanted, rejected…'

'Of course you did,' Polly framed, still in shock from what he had just told her, her every belief about his first marriage violently turned on its head and her heart going out to him.

'And that is why you were right to accuse me of a lack of enthusiasm on the day we married.' Rashad surveyed her with anguished dark eyes, full of guilt and regret. 'You said you wanted it all so I am telling you everything. I knew it was my duty to remarry but I *dreaded* the thought of being a husband again. I had nothing but bad memories of the first experience and my expectations were very low—'

Polly unfroze with difficulty and sat down on legs

that felt weak, not quite sure she was strong enough to take the honesty she had asked him to give her because what he was now telling her was beginning to hurt. 'I can understand that,' she said limply.

'I was completely selfish in my behaviour. I was bitter and angry. I felt trapped. And then you *saved* me,' he framed harshly. 'I did nothing to deserve you, Polly. I am not worthy of the happiness you have brought into my life.'

Reeling from that 'trapped' word that had pierced her like a knife, Polly studied him in confusion. 'You're talking about the baby?' she pressed. 'That's made you happy?'

His black brows drew together. 'No, I'm talking about you. Our baby is a wonderful gift and I am very grateful to be so blessed but my happiness is entirely based on having you in my life…'

'Oh,' Polly mumbled in surprise.

Rashad crossed the rug between them and dropped down on his knees at her feet to look levelly at her with insistent dark golden eyes. 'I think I probably fell in love with you the first time I saw you. It was like an electric shock. I had never felt anything like it before and of course I didn't recognise it for what it was. It was love but I thought it was lust because I didn't know any better…'

'Love?' Polly almost whispered. 'You *love* me?'

'Madly, insanely,' Rashad extended raggedly. 'I can't bear to have you out of my sight. I think about you all the time. The thought of losing you terrifies me.

And yet I have made mistake after mistake with you and done nothing to earn your regard—'

Polly grinned at him, the happiness he insisted she had brought him bubbling up through her in receipt of such an impassioned declaration. She definitely loved him and loved him all the more for abandoning his reserve and his formality and his pride to convince her of the sincerity of his feelings for her. 'I felt that electric shock thing too,' she told him teasingly. 'Every time I laid eyes on you, I felt like an infatuated schoolgirl. Why do you think I married you? I married you because I fell in love with you…'

*'Truly?'* Rashad exclaimed in ego-boosting amazement as he sprang upright and stepped back for an instant simply to savour her beautiful glowing face.

'Truly,' Polly confirmed with a helpless beaming smile of encouragement.

Rashad scooped her up very, very gently, being mindful of her sore hip, and carried her into their bedroom to lay her down on the bed. He shed his jacket and tie and settled down beside her to ease her fully into his arms. 'I love you so much, *habibti*. But I am forbidden to do anything more than hold you close for a few days,' he admitted in a roughened voice. 'Yet it is enough to still have that right, believe me.'

Ignoring the hint of soreness from her stiff hip, Polly squirmed round in the circle of his arms to face him. She ran wondering fingers across a high masculine cheekbone and marvelled at the silky black lashes semi-veiling his adoring eyes. 'I think a kiss is in order…and I'm expecting a real award winner of a kiss,' she warned him cheekily.

'I will try to deliver,' Rashad groaned, gazing down at her clear blue eyes with fervent appreciation. 'I always try to deliver—'

'Well, you were pretty nifty in the baby stakes,' she conceded.

'Nifty together…' He nibbled at her full lower lip and she closed her eyes, literally so happy she felt that she should be floating on high, but then she wouldn't have let go of Rashad for anything because his lean, powerful body felt so very good against hers. And they might be different and he might be much more old-fashioned than he was willing to admit, but she knew that they complemented each other beautifully.

# EPILOGUE

'I CAN'T BELIEVE that after all this time we still haven't found Gemma.' Polly sighed and shot a pained glance at her sister, Ellie. 'I mean, it's been months and we still know next to nothing about our long-lost sibling!'

'Well, we know that she had a tough childhood and she has no roots to cling to,' Ellie argued in a more measured tone. 'We can also assume that she moves around a lot because we never seem to catch up with her and we know she works in *really* dead-end jobs. That's a lot more than we knew about Gemma starting out.'

Polly nodded reluctantly. 'True…but what if she doesn't *want* to know about us?' she asked worriedly. 'We've advertised in the papers, notified social services that we're looking, informed everyone who has known her in the past that we want to find her—'

'We have to be patient,' Ellie cut in firmly. 'And that's not a trait you possess although, heaven knows, you possess everything else.'

'What's that supposed to mean?' Polly prompted.

Ellie rolled her eyes. 'Movie-star-handsome King as

husband—check. An adoring population who think you can walk on water—check. Constant sunshine overhead, royal palace—check. Loving grandparents—check. An adorable baby son… Yes, I'm talking about you, you little darling!' She stopped to speak to Karim, who crawled across the rug to his aunt to grab the toy she was extending. 'I suppose you're already planning on extending the family?'

Polly flushed. 'Not just yet. I'd like Karim to be a little older before we try again. I'm not a baby machine, Ellie. I mean, look at you, you don't even date—'

'I'm too busy working. Between my shifts and the hospital and the exams I don't have time for a man. Anyway, most of them are a waste of space,' her redheaded sister contended. 'No, I like my life just the way it is. I eat what I like, go where I like, do as I like and that's important to me. The minute a man enters the equation, all your choices start disappearing—'

'And you still have no plans to look into your background?' Polly pressed.

Ellie sighed. 'Actually I'm taking a couple of months off once I complete my residency and I'm planning on heading to Italy and doing a little discreet detective work—'

'Oh, that's great!' Polly gushed approvingly. 'Will you tell me your father's name now?'

Ellie groaned. 'The reason I didn't tell you the name before is that I got given two names—'

Polly's eyes widened. *'Two?'*

'Yes,' Ellie confirmed drily. 'Two names. Obviously our mother didn't know which man fathered me and, sleaziest of all, the men were *brothers*. I've done some research. One of the men is alive, the other dead. The living one is a wealthy retired art collector who lives in a *palazzo* outside Florence—his brother passed away years ago.'

Polly stared at her sister in consternation, belatedly grasping why the younger woman had been so silent on the topic of her own unknown father and background. 'Oh, dear…I'm so sorry—'

'No, you got the fairy tale…the military hero father who married our mother…and I got a pair of dead-beat dads,' Ellie mocked with wry humour. 'I'm glad it worked out that way. I can handle messy reality better than you can.'

'I could come to Italy with you!' Polly proffered in dismay. 'Be your support.'

'No, you'd wilt like a flower out of water deprived of Rashad and Karim,' Ellie forecast drily. 'And that's if your husband would even *let* you go—'

'Rashad doesn't tell me what to do—'

'No, but he hates it when you're away even for a couple of days,' Ellie reminded her wryly. 'You came over to see me at Christmas and Rashad was on the phone every five minutes. You actually fell asleep talking to him one night. Having you to stay was like separating a pair of lovelorn teenagers. It's unhealthy to be so attached to each other…'

Polly simply laughed, knowing that Ellie had never been in love. Nothing came between Ellie and the medical career she adored. But Polly had never had that burning ambition for a career and her wants and needs were satisfied by her family circle and her public role as the Queen of Dharia. She was always very busy, particularly since the birth of their son a year earlier. They had a nanny to help with Karim's care but both Polly and Rashad spent a great deal of time with their son. Polly wanted Karim to know how much he was loved and Rashad was determined to play a daily part in his child's routine.

'It's so beautiful here,' Ellie remarked dreamily, contemplating the star-shaped pool into which water flowed endlessly. Lush trees and luxuriant foliage softened the carved stone arches and pillars of the palace walls that surrounded the courtyard. 'You saw this place first, didn't you? Maybe that's why you fell for Rashad.'

'You are such a cynic, Ellie,' Rashad declared with amusement as he joined them.

Karim loosed a yell and crawled at speed across the tiles to greet his father. Rashad chuckled and bent down to scoop up the little boy and kiss him with an unashamed love that touched Polly's heart. The man she had married had slowly learned to loosen up and show his true colours. His passion in bed was now equally matched by the depth of his affection. He said that she had changed him but Polly believed he had changed himself. He was happy now and it showed in the ease of his brilliant smile and the burnished glow of his dark eyes.

'Well, was it the palace that cast a spell over you... or me?' Rashad teased, gazing down at his wife as she moved to his side.

'If you two are going to turn all lovey-dovey, I'm going upstairs for a shower,' Ellie announced in a deflating tone.

'Lovey-dovey?' Rashad queried, walking Polly out of the courtyard with an arm draped round her shoulder and Karim tucked below the other.

'Drippy…mushy,' she translated. 'Ellie hates that stuff.'

'Are we…drippy?' Rashad enquired with a pained look.

'Probably sometimes,' she said fondly. 'Who cares as long as we're happy?'

'I am not drippy,' Rashad proclaimed with distaste as Polly removed Karim from his arms and settled their son in his cot for his nap.

Karim howled as if he had been abandoned in the street and Rashad hovered worriedly.

'He's fine. He always does that. He's just like you, very resilient and he tries it on sometimes. Don't let him think you're going to lift him again,' Polly warned as she dragged Rashad out of the nursery again.

'Tough love…right?' Rashad guessed, wincing as Karim kept on crying.

'Wait,' Polly instructed in the corridor.

When he was deprived of an audience, the crying stopped and their son began to talk to himself quite happily.

Rashad smiled, much relieved by the development.

'Yeah, you're really drippy!' Polly teased with satisfaction, walking into their bedroom.

'I'm not. I'm a concerned parent who doesn't like to hear my child cry,' Rashad argued.

'And I'm what? The evil mother who left him to cry?'

'No, you're the wonderful wife who is giving me an hour of alone time with you before dinner,' Rashad said with a wicked grin as he began stripping off his clothes with alacrity. 'This is yet another reason why I love you so much.'

Polly ran appreciative fingers up over his rock-hard abdomen and watched his muscles ripple, dry-mouthed with admiration. 'I'm greedy… I always make time for you.'

He crushed her lips beneath his with a heady moan of pleasure. 'You taste so good, *habibti.*'

Her body was sparking like a fizzing firework, eager for the ignition point of his. No, they hadn't lost their passion for each other. Admittedly her pregnancy had slowed them down a bit in the final months but she had rediscovered her energy after Karim's birth and the nanny had helped by doing the night feeds. They rolled across the bed kissing and exchanging sounds of mutual love and longing and, as always, it was amazing. They lay together afterwards, wrapped in each other and temporary satiety.

Rashad ran his fingers through her hair, stared down at her peaceful face with true devotion in his gaze. 'You really are the best thing that ever happened to me,' he told her gruffly. 'When I wake up in the morning and see you beside me, my heart lifts and I feel that I can cope with anything.'

'I love you too,' Polly whispered with shining eyes.

And he kissed her again and dinner was served late and Ellie gave her sister a withering glance.

'And you looked at me when I said you were like teenagers?' she quipped.

'Wait until you fall in love,' Polly urged.

'Not going to happen. I'm too sensible,' her sister assured her confidently.

\* \* \* \* \*

*If you enjoyed this story,*
*don't miss Lynne Graham's other great reads!*
*THE GREEK'S CHRISTMAS BRIDE*
*THE ITALIAN'S CHRISTMAS CHILD*
*BOUGHT FOR THE GREEK'S REVENGE*
*THE SICILIAN'S STOLEN SON*
*LEONETTI'S HOUSEKEEPER BRIDE*
*Available now!*

*Also look out for the second book in*
*Lynne's BRIDES FOR THE TAKING trilogy,*
*coming in April 2017!*

# MILLS & BOON®

# MODERN™

**POWER, PASSION AND IRRESISTIBLE TEMPTATION**

# MILLS & BOON®

## EXCLUSIVE EXTRACT

Raul Di Savo desires more than Lydia Hayward's
body—his seduction will stop his rival buying her!
Raul's expert touch awakens Lydia to irresistible
pleasure, but his game of revenge forces
Lydia to leave… until an unexpected
consequence binds them forever!

*Read on for a sneak preview of*
*THE INNOCENT'S SECRET BABY*

Somehow Lydia was back against the wall with Raul's
hands either side of her head.

She put her hands up to his chest and felt him solid
beneath her palms and she just felt him there a moment
and then looked up to his eyes.

His mouth moved in close and as it did she stared
right into his eyes.

She could feel heat hover between their mouths in a
slow tease before they first met.

Then they met.

And all that had been missing was suddenly there.

Yet, the gentle pressure his mouth exerted, though
blissful, caused a mire of sensations until the gentleness
of his kiss was no longer enough.

A slight inhale, a hitch in her breath and her lips
parted, just a little, and he slipped his tongue in.

The moan she made went straight to his groin.

At first taste she was his and he knew it for her hands

moved to the back of his head and he kissed her as hard back as her fingers demanded.

More so even.

His tongue was wicked and her fingers tightened in his thick hair and she could feel the wall cold and hard against her shoulders.

It was the middle of Rome just after six and even down a side street there was no real hiding from the crowds.

Lydia didn't care.

He slid one arm around her waist to move her body away from the wall and closer into his, so that her head could fall backwards.

If there was a bed, she would be on it.

If there was a room they would close the door.

Yet there wasn't and so he halted them, but only their lips.

Their bodies were heated and close and he looked her right in the eye. His mouth was wet from hers and his hair a little messed from her fingers.

*Don't miss*
THE INNOCENT'S SECRET BABY,
By Carol Marinelli

Available March 2017
www.millsandboon.co.uk

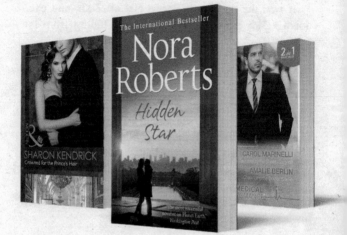